Heart of a Highlander
Real Men Wear Kilts

by

Maxine Mansfield

Heart of a Highlander

Contact Information: info@thewildrosepress.com

Cover Art by *Diana Carlile*

The Wild Rose Press, Inc.
PO Box 708
Adams Basin, NY 14410-0708

Visit us at www.thewilderroses.com

Publishing History
First Scarlet Rose Edition, 2019
Print ISBN 978-1-5092-2520-0
Digital ISBN 978-1-5092-2521-7

Published in the United States of America

**Sometimes it takes more
than one lifetime to find true love…**

The priest looped the end of the swatch of plaid about their wrists for a third time. "Will ye share each other's pain and burdens and laughter and tears as ye travel through this life?"

Again, Ian nodded, no longer trusting himself to even try and speak.

Just as before, Aila said, "Aye," loudly and clearly.

Once again, the priest looped the fabric about their wrists, but this time he tied the two ends into a secure knot. "As much as Ian and Aila have consented ta be joined in marriage before God and these witnesses, it is the decree of the church that their lives be long, their loins fruitful, and their days be filled with plenty."

He turned in a circle with his arms stretched wide before once more facing Ian and Aila. "May the elements be always with ye. From the East, may the air breath inta ye a purity of heart along with the rising of the sun each new day. May the South, with its fire, fill ye with passion even during the darkest of winter nights. May the water from the West give ye peace even in times of great sorrow. And from the North and its element of earth, may yer lands feed ye and yer people, and may ye always prosper."

And with that, Ian Mackay, former staff sergeant from almost four hundred years in the future and from itty-bitty Johnsville, Ohio, was now a married laird in the 1643 highlands of Scotland.

Dedication

For my wonderful nephew, Josh,
and all those like him who towed the line, walked the
walk, and did what should never be asked of another
human being. Thank you for your service. God bless.
And I'm so glad you finally found your way back
home.

The End...Or Is It?
In the blink of an eye life can end.
What once was familiar disappears like the wind.
In the space of a heartbeat the world can shift.
What once was unwanted can now become a gift.
In a split second reality can fade.
And in its place a new beginning be made.

What comes after, what came before?
Time becomes irrelevant
when you walk through that door.
Death is a beginning when life is at an end.
It can be your greatest foe or your dearest of friends.
But do nae worry, for ye'll never truly be alone.
For that death finds us all is a fact verra well known.

Chapter One

Present day early spring
Johnsville, Ohio

Ian Mackay floored his '98 Dodge Dakota pickup and allowed the brisk March wind to do what not much else could these days. Speed and icy-cold air buffeting his face were about the only things that remotely made him feel alive anymore. A condition he spent most days fluctuating between thankfulness and regret.

Even after three long years, multiple self-help groups, and more shrinks than he'd like to remember, he still couldn't begin to accept what had happened in Afghanistan and move on with his life. After all, what right did he have to still be drawing a breath when so many no longer were?

Why had his life gone so horribly wrong? He'd followed all the rules and done everything expected of him. He'd been quarterback for his high school football team, the Northmor-Knights, and proudly worn the black and gold. And he'd been in the top ten percent of his graduating class, which had made both his mamma and papa proud. And though sorely tempted, he hadn't once played hooky or come home drunk, let alone done drugs.

He'd even done his due diligence and helped plant row after row after fucking corn right alongside his father each year. He'd slopped those smelly-ass hogs every single morning, and he'd gathered at least a thousand eggs in his lifetime. All in the hopes that when he was grown he'd never have to work a piece of ground again. There had to be something more than being a fucking farmer to look forward to. There just had to be.

It wasn't as if Ian begrudged his father the profession he'd chosen after serving his country, for he hadn't. It was that it simply hadn't been what he'd wanted to do with his life.

He'd even gone to church each and every Sunday morning and listened to the preacher's sermons, and at least pretended he wanted to be there. Granted, it was usually after trying fruitlessly to cross the line with Amy Lynn Havisham on any given Saturday night. But then what teenage boy didn't try to seduce the panties right off a pretty young thing when and if the opportunity arose?

He'd made his parents so happy when he'd graduated high school with honors, and then again when he enlisted in the Marines as his father and grandfather had before him.

Well, one thing was for certain. He wasn't making anyone happy or proud anymore. These days, his parents glanced his way with worry or fear in their eyes most days, even anger sometimes, and worst of all, that fucking never-ending pity.

And here he'd thought he'd mapped his life out so perfectly. A life that had included his best friend Danny. They'd been inseparable from the very first day of kindergarten. Where one was seen, so was the other. If one was in trouble, then the other was surely just as guilty. They'd laughed and played, planned and schemed, and dreamed of a life much different than that of simple farm boys.

Danny had been the brother of Ian's heart.

He was irreplaceable.

But irreplaceable or not, he was still just as gone.

They'd both intended to serve their country as long as their country had need of them. And when they were done, they would come home together. They would join the local police force and keep all those they loved safe. Never again would they plow a field, plant a row of corn, slop a hog, or gather another fucking egg. Instead, they'd find themselves a couple of pretty, young things who were willing to settle down and raise a passel of kids with them. Even if it was just in small town Amish country, Johnsville, Ohio.

Ian sighed as he pressed his foot harder on the gas pedal. If life had taught him anything, it was that things rarely went as planned.

If only he could go back eleven years to his eighteen-year-old self and warn him. Not that he wouldn't have joined the service and done his duty, because he still would've. He just would've done it differently. He didn't for a minute regret his two tours of duty in Iraq, or even his last tour in Afghanistan.

Well, at least he hadn't regretted most of it.

But that last tour, really, just that last day of his tour in Afghanistan, he would change the outcome of that day if he could.

A staff sergeant protects his men. A staff sergeant guides his men. A staff sergeant leads his men. A staff sergeant does not get a good portion of his fucking squad killed, and especially not his best friend in the whole wide world. But he had gotten them killed, and nothing could ever change that fact or what living with the knowledge of his actions—really his lack of action—had done to him.

He cranked up the radio until the sound of the country singer's voice drowned out his morbid thoughts. He floored the gas once more. Speed. He just needed more speed.

No, he couldn't change a thing that had happened. Even now, his pickup was loaded down with seed corn for the spring crops and feed for those nasty-ass hogs. And any minute now, he'd be back on the farm, doing the only thing he was any good for anymore.

Men with diagnosed Post Traumatic Stress Disorder didn't pass psych-evals for the police academy. Men who'd barely managed to survive being blown to smithereens didn't pass physical agility tests either. And there were no pretty, little small-town girls waiting for him to get home, let alone looking to start a family. Especially not Amy Lynn Havisham.

Hell, she wouldn't even speak to him anymore.

When he did work up the nerve to venture out for a drink or a little female companionship, what happened then? He more often than not struck out completely or ended up just paying a professional for her time. For the moment some sweet little farmer's daughter looked him straight in the eye, they quickly turned away. Afghanistan had changed him, and they knew it.

There was something dark about him now, something just a little off center. It was as if they'd glimpsed the insanity he fought so hard to hide. Or more likely, the low-down, piece-of-shit loser he'd come to realize probably described him best.

But then perhaps the female population of

Johnsville, Ohio was right about him. Perhaps his soul was so damaged it was beyond redemption. Perhaps that was what happened when he let his best friend die when he could've prevented it by being a heartbeat faster, by not fucking hesitating.

Perhaps this sorry excuse for an existence was his just due for not pulling the trigger a heartbeat sooner.

The sun was just setting as Ian barreled up the oh-so familiar steep hill of the icy gravel road. The same hill he'd driven thousands of times. Five more minutes and he'd be home. Five more minutes and there'd be seed corn to unload and hogs to feed and meds to take and another long, lonely night to endure.

He closed his eyes and prayed. "Not tonight. Please, God, don't make me relive it again tonight. I'm tired. So very, very tired."

When he opened his eyes, all thoughts of future nightmares fled, for coming straight toward him was a real live horror. At the top of the hill, right in the middle of the road, was an all too familiar sight. It was a black, squat, slow-moving Amish buggy, and at this rate, he was going much too fast to avoid hitting it. If the terror on the young girl's face behind the reins of that great big four-legged horse of hers was any indication, she knew it, too.

But he had to give her credit, she tried to swerve anyway.

The Amish girl jerked hard on her reins, and the horse spooked. The chestnut-brown mare's nostrils flared as it picked up speed instead, its hooves pounding the pavement, its eyes wide with fear, and its head whipping back and forth. If he didn't do something to prevent what was about to happen, and do it now, the girl, her horse, and probably even himself were all going to die this day.

Self-preservation and adrenaline took over.

Seconds zoomed by as he jerked the steering wheel sharply to the right, and though his tires skidded as they came in contact with the icy gravel, he still had no problem seeing clearly the look of surprise on the young girl's face as she, her horse, and her buggy slipped right past him without so much as a scratch.

The very beginning of a smile lifted the corners of his mouth. After all the mistakes he'd made in his life, he'd finally managed to do one thing right.

But the skid and the heavy weight of the seed corn and feed in the back of his truck prevented him from correcting, and over the embankment Ian flipped.

Where moments ago, time had flashed by at the speed of light, now it all but stood still.

The first flip of his truck and the windshield shattered. Shards of glass flying in every direction like a thousand tiny diamonds suspended upon the wind. Twice and Ian found he could almost count each individual clump of cold dead grass as they meandered past his line of vision. Then a third time and the glittering rays of a cold March sun reflecting off the icy-cold ground was the last sight he saw. For when the '98 Dodge pickup truck finally came to rest, twenty-nine-year-old Ian Mackay, decorated war hero, son of mid-west farmers from itty-bitty Johnsville, Ohio, breathed no more.

Or so he thought.

****

"Enough lolly-gagging around, lad. Open your eyes and get yourself out of there. I don't have time to

7

be standing around here all day."

"What the hell?" Ian slowly obeyed and tried his best to do as the strange voice asked, but a sudden wave of dizziness prevented him from making much progress. He took two deep breaths and tried again. Glancing around, he found himself upside down but still securely strapped inside his truck. He wiggled and fought with the seatbelt latch, but it wouldn't give.

"I seem to be stuck." He wiggled again. "A little help would be greatly appreciated."

The stranger with tousled brown hair, wire-rimmed glasses, and wearing what looked to be a white robe of some kind sighed. "I suppose it wouldn't hurt to help this one time."

The man snapped his fingers, and Ian suddenly found himself right side up and standing beside his overturned truck. A wave of nausea overcame him as he quickly dusted off his jeans and checked himself for injuries. He was surprised not to find a single scratch.

"Wow." He blew out a quick breath. "That sure was lucky, though I'm going to have a devil of a time getting my truck back up on its wheels I'm afraid." He glanced around. "Where's the little Amish girl I almost hit? I need to make sure she's all right."

The man in the white robe looking thingy sighed again. "The girl is of no consequence."

Irritation filled Ian. He appreciated the stranger's help, but at the same time, he didn't appreciate the man's rudeness. He turned and headed up toward the road. "Thank you, but whether you find the girl of consequence or not, I need to check on her. I'm pretty sure I scared the living shit out of her, and that was never my intention."

The stranger tapped Ian on the shoulder, and when he turned to see what the man was about, his eyes followed the direction the stranger was pointing. There stood the young Amish girl, in her plain black dress with its plain white apron, and her plain black bonnet, tears streaming down her face. She was staring into the front seat of Ian's pickup and the carnage within.

Bile rose in his throat and threatened to spew forth as he realized just what, or really just who, she was staring at.

It was him, or at least what was left of him. His body still hung upside down. His bloody face was twisted at an impossible angle, his blue eyes still wide open, and his already red hair growing redder with every passing moment. His broken limbs hung limply askew and at odd angles. He had no doubt he'd never play football, or anything else, with those arms and legs again.

Like a horror movie, he tried to look away and couldn't. Seed corn littered the ground, and a fine dusting of hog's feed mixed with drying blood coated a good part of his truck.

Ian felt sorry for the Amish girl. Though she was probably somewhere between sixteen and eighteen, she was still much too young to be exposed to such a horrific sight. He tried to place a hand on her shoulder to offer comfort, but it went right through her as if he wasn't even there.

Realization hit him, and he gagged. "I'm dead. That's really me, or what's left of me anyway, still in that truck, isn't it? And I'm really and truly dead, aren't I?"

"Let's not be so melodramatic, shall we," the

stranger said. "Of course, you're dead. What else did you expect to happen when you were driving like Mario Andretti on an icy gravel road instead of a proper speedway? It was only a matter of time."

Ian shook his head. "There must be some mistake. I don't feel dead."

The stranger sniffed. "Oh, and I suppose you're an expert on death now, too? After a whole five minutes or so." He sighed once more. "Let me make this perfectly clear because I am a very busy man and I don't have all of eternity to waste chit-chatting with the likes of you."

The man took off his wire-rimmed glasses, cleaned them on the sleeve of his robe, and then placed them back on his face. "You are dead as the proverbial doornail. Dead as a mashed flat bug on the windshield of an eighteen-wheeler. Just as dead as the Lost Sea Scrolls, and certainly as dead as those souls from your squad unfortunate enough to be riding with you that day."

Ian gulped. "Wow, that's a low blow. Who are you, anyway, and if I'm really and truly dead, then how is it you can see me? And shouldn't I be moving on or going towards the light or something?" He gulped again. "I don't want to be here when others start showing up, like my parents."

The stranger shuffled his feet and stuffed his hands deep into the pockets of his robe. "Let's not worry about who I am just yet. What's more important is I'm here to offer you a proposition. And you're right, normally you would've moved on by now, but even the boss agrees with me on this one. At least on principal, so we have other plans for you."

"Plans? What plans? And who's your boss," Ian

asked.

The stranger took his right hand out of his pocket and pointed skyward. "You know, The Boss, The Creator, The Big Kahuna, Buddha, Jehovah, the Messiah, God, or whatever else you humans may choose to call Him today. And as far as what we need you to do, just remember, it wasn't really my fault. Any Fate in their right mind would've done the same thing given the same circumstances."

Ian scoffed. "God needs me? I doubt that. He's all powerful, from what I've always been told. He doesn't need anyone or anything."

"You'd be surprised," the stranger whispered. "Just because He's all knowing and all seeing doesn't mean He hasn't had His share of mishaps. Yet He still blames me for a rookie mistake I made a long time ago. My one and only I can tell you. Well, kind of my one and only anyway.

"And not that I'd ever bring up any of His accidents to His face, mind you, like He does me every chance He gets. You don't honestly believe He meant to create the blob-fish, for instance, or the proboscis monkey, do you? Oh, but He's more than a little sensitive if anyone brings up anything about those two. Not to mention the homely warthog or the star-nosed mole. But let me make one itsy-bitsy mistake and I never get to live it down."

Ian shook his head. "And what happens if I don't want to do whatever it is you say needs doing? What happens to me then?"

The stranger chuckled. "Humans, you never fail to entertain. What happens to you? What do you think happens to you? You'd go onto your judgment, of course. But if you'd by chance like the opportunity to go back and take another shot, I just might be able to arrange that. You know what I mean, don't you? Wouldn't you like another chance to try and change what happened to Danny and the others who died that day in Afghanistan? Because, even though The Boss chooses not to precisely know how I go about getting things done, having a second chance at that day in Afghanistan is what I'm offering if you're willing to do this one little favor for me."

Ian didn't trust the stranger, but if anyone would be willing to give him another chance to save Danny and the others, it was a chance he couldn't and wouldn't pass up. "What exactly is the job? Just about anything's gotta be better than farming."

"It's simple really." The stranger smiled. "Easy-peasy, piece of cake. All you need do is go back into the past of one of your very distant relatives and give the man back the life he stupidly threw away much too soon. Like I said, when a Fate does make a mistake, it's usually a doozy. The first Ian Mackay wasn't supposed to die when or how he did.

"Almost four hundred years later and the Big Guy is still brooding about what happened afterwards. Ian Mackay wasn't the only person affected the night he died, you know? Time really is like a ripple upon a pond, and the consequences of one's actions can be very far reaching indeed."

Ian's stomach did a flip-flop. "And just how am I supposed to stop this other Ian Mackay guy from dying?"

The stranger pulled what appeared to be a smart-phone looking thingy from his left pocket and started pushing buttons. "You can't prevent him from dying, silly. That's a done deal. But we can slip your soul into his body, and you can become him right after his own death. And if you do this, you just might be able to prevent what followed."

Ian took a deep breath. "So, you're saying if I go back in time and take up where this other guy left off, then I'll be given a chance to change what happened to Danny and the other men I lost in Afghanistan?" He held out his hand to shake on it. "Sign me up."

The stranger didn't say a word or shake his hand but continued to push buttons on his contraption.

The air around Ian began to shimmer, and time and space itself shifted as he felt himself being lifted up and away.

"Wait," he yelled across the expanse. "You never did tell me who you are or where I'm going."

Just a whisper of a voice reached Ian's ears a moment before he found himself sucked into the swirling vortex of a void. "You'll see in a moment where you're going, and as for who I am, I'm Tobias Moiré, third generation event manipulator, of course. But you're free to call me by my everyday moniker if you like. I, sir, am Fate."

Chapter Two

Late April 1643
Skelbo Castle, Northern Scotland

Saints be praised. Ian Mackay was stone cold dead.

Not that Aila Gordon had a hand in his demise, for she hadn't. All she'd done was step inside his chamber to check on the drunken fool.

She stared down at the unmoving body of the highlander and shuddered. She couldn't help herself. Though she'd definitely not wished to marry a man who was an enemy of her clan come the morrow, she hadn't wished him dead either. Well, not precisely anyway. Perhaps she'd wished him to perdition a time or two in the last few hours, but she really hadn't meant it. Not really.

It simply wasn't fair, even in death, and even lying face down in a pool of his own vomit, Ian Mackay was still much too much of a braw highlander for his or anyone else's good. She couldn't help herself. She turned his head to the side, even though he was no longer breathing and brushed a lock of midnight black hair from his wet cheek. No man, not even a murdering, thieving, lying, cheating, no good Mackay should be found in such a disgraceful state.

Her traitorous fingers itched to gently stoke that cheek.

It really, truly wasn't fair. In death, his black as

night hair still curled playfully about his ears. And his cheek still looked so caressingly soft, even with its day's growth of stubble. And though his eyes were now closed, as if he were simply sleeping, and his long lashes rested gently against that soft cheek, it didn't for a moment stop her from remembering how deep a blue those eyes were. Just as deep and just as stormy blue as the ocean not far from the northern Scottish castle walls outside this very chamber.

No, it was not fair. No man had the right to be that…bonny. Especially when she herself was not.

But then, what right did any Mackay man have to be so handsome? When, in reality, all the men from his clan should be sprouting horns and scales so that normal people like her and her kinfolk, could see them for what they truly were and not be fooled by their charms like King Charles had obviously been. The very same king who'd ordered her, a Gordon and the sister of one of Ian Mackay's greatest enemies, to marry the beast, just to put an end to a stupid feud.

She scoffed. As if a marriage to her, or any Gordon as far as that was concerned, could accomplish such a thing.

The Gordons, well, really the clan Sutherland in which her kinfolk were a big part, had been warring with the Mackays for more than a few generations. It was tradition, and neither side was even sure anymore what or who had started it and didn't really care.

Aila glanced down at Ian again and sighed. She'd only come to his chamber to make sure the man had actually made it here in one piece. After all, when he'd left the great hall below, she had been surprised the idiot could even stand up straight let alone walk.

Castle Skelbo's *uisge beatha* was well known throughout the land for being some of the strongest whisky made in all of Scotland. It hadn't ever killed anyone before, though. But then, there was a first time for everything.

She poked him with the toe of her slipper once more for good measure, and just like the three times before, he didn't even twitch. Perhaps he shouldn't have tried to drink her brother under the table. Better men than him had failed, many times before.

Aila shuddered again. Though she truly hadn't wished to marry anyone, let alone a Mackay, she kind of regretted the fact she wasn't going to have a wedding to worry about come morning, let alone a bedding afterwards. Especially since Ian Mackay was so bonny to look upon. And that was just the parts she'd seen.

She turned to leave but lingered as she slowly faced him once more. Curiosity got the better of her, and Aila's cheeks heated as she toed the edge of his kilt upward until his manhood became visible. Lord help her, but she was fascinated. It was long and thick and sadly, just like its master, now lifeless.

She should hurry down the stairs this very moment. She should tell her brother and Ian's kinsmen the man was dead. After all, she couldn't just leave him like this, could she?

Yet she hesitated once more.

If she sounded the alarm, would the Mackays think she'd somehow taken advantage of Ian's drunken state and killed him herself? Would the bad blood between the two clans escalate? Would more lives be lost?

Aila couldn't take that chance.

Instead, she turned on her heel and fled to the

safety of her own chamber. It would be much better for one of his own men to find him dead from excessive drink come morning. Much better indeed, for all their sakes.

****

Ian gasped and coughed long and loud as he choked on a lung full of something gross and acidic. His throat burned, his head pounded, and every muscle in his body felt as if he'd been beaten to within an inch of his life. Bile spewed forth and ran down the already wet front of whatever it was he was wearing.

"What the hell," he managed to squeak out before another coughing fit wracked his frame.

He could hear the Tobias Moiré Fate guy tapping his foot on the stone floor nearby.

"Seriously, dude, what the hell?" Ian's fingers and toes tingled as if his limbs had fallen asleep, and a cold he'd never known the likes of before, not even in the deepest, darkest Ohio winter night, chilled him to the very marrow of his bones.

He shivered uncontrollably.

Tobias sighed. "What did you expect? You've just been transported through time and into a body that was dead only moments ago."

Ian coughed again, and his eyes watered. "Oh, I don't know what I expected when my life ended— trumpets, marching bands, angelic choirs? How the hell was I supposed to know what it would be like to suddenly inhabit some other guy's dead body?"

Tobias sighed once more. "I really don't have time for this. I'm not even the usual Fate for your particular part of the world. That's my Cousin Norbert's job. But since you're ending up in my part of the world and since it was originally my mistake, I felt I'd better handle this matter myself. So please do be quiet for a moment and listen. When I finish, you may ask any questions you might have, if there's time, that is."

The old man moved until he stood directly before Ian. "Your consciousness is now firmly implanted within the body of this Ian Mackay, who has been promised a small castle and holdings of his own near the mid-northern coast of Scotland. But only if he actually goes through with the marriage to one Aila Gordon. Who just so happens to be the sister of one of his clan's greatest enemies.

"You are now in the year 1643 in the Scottish Highlands. Charles the First is king of both England and Scotland. There is a battle brewing between the Royalists and the Parliamentarians, and the entire country is on the verge of war and famine. But then, this is Scotland, and on just about any given day, they are on the verge of war and famine."

Ian placed his hands on unfamiliar hips and shook his head as an overwhelming feeling of dread seeped deep into his soul. "What the hell have I agreed to?"

"It's simple really," Fate continued. "Your job is to marry the girl, claim the castle, and do what you can to make life bearable for the people who were counting on Laird Ian Mackay to save them. Do this, and your wish will be granted. That is all."

Tobias Moiré, third generation event manipulator, began to flicker in and out and shimmer.

"Wait, wait, wait," Ian gasped. His military training took over as fear edged in. He couldn't take on a mission with no information. He needed a plan of action. "Where do you think you're going? You can't just leave me here. I don't know anything about this country except that some of my distant relatives were from here. I sure as hell don't know its history. And I don't know this Ian Mackay guy or a single thing about 1643 Scotland, for God's sake. What was the man like? Who was he? What else happened in this time and in this place? What do I do first? How do I talk to these people? How don't I talk? What do I wear? I have a million questions at least."

Tobias continued to flicker. "I will be available if and when you truly need me, but I can't stay here with you and hold your hand. As I've said before, I am a very busy man. Tap into the other Ian Mackay's memories. They can tell you a great deal. Memories are like energy. They don't die even when their host does. They simply become part of the universe. As far as talking, you are already speaking Gaelic without even realizing it, but I do suggest you throw in the occasional yae or nae, and perhaps a lad or lassie every now and then. As for what you should do first, I suggest you take yourself down to the loch and bathe. You, sir, are covered in vomit and stink."

And with that, Fate completely disappeared.

"Oh my fucking god, what've I gotten myself in to?" Ian shuddered.

Panic threatened to engulf him, and he fought the need to curl into himself and hide. Instead, he took deep calming breaths to stave off the terror while ignoring sweaty palms and a pounding heart. He could do this. Really, he could. He'd done two tours of duty in Iraq and one in Afghanistan. How hard could 1643 Scotland be?

With his back to the door Ian quickly glanced

around the small, dark room and took inventory of his surroundings. Not that there was adequate light in order to assess much of anything. Embers burnt down low in a stone fireplace against the wall to his right while subtle streaks of moonlight from a small window-like opening directly in front of him cast a glow upon the only real piece of furniture to be seen. It was a bed, or at least he thought it was a bed. What looked like a straw-stuffed mattress was covered with dark furs on a low wooden platform of some kind.

He turned in a circle. What the fuck was he supposed to do now? Fate had told him that he stunk and needed a bath, and without even breathing in deeply, that was one fact Ian couldn't argue. But what and where exactly was a loch? It had to be some kind of body of water if people bathed in it. Which meant it had to be outside whatever structure he was now in.

So outside was where he needed to go, because though he'd paid only enough attention in history classes to get a passing grade, he knew that in the year 1643, there was no indoor plumbing or hot running water anywhere. Especially not in the most northern highlands of Scotland.

Damn, cold ass water in the dead of night in a strange country. This certainly wasn't starting out well, was it?

He turned and grasped the handle of the wooden door. Cold and dark or not, if he wanted to ever get his friend and his men back, he'd better get started.

****

Aila yawned, stretched, and smiled before snuggling back down into the warmth of her fur-covered bed once again. Bright rays of spring sunshine flittering across her wall told her the morning was well on its way, but she didn't care. There was no longer any reason to rise early. There would be no wedding to a Mackay, or anyone else on this day.

Then another thought struck, and her smile quickly faded. Would King Charles force another of the Mackay clan upon her once he was informed that Ian was dead? And if he did choose another, what kind of man would that one be?

She worried her lip.

Not that she wasn't happy her intended was dead, for she was, but simply because he was a Mackay and not for any other reason. Though Ian Mackay's linage was flawed and he belonged to the wrong clan didn't mean the man hadn't had his share of charms. For one, he'd been extremely handsome. So handsome, as a matter of fact, that it had been almost uncomfortable to gaze upon him for very long. And his voice... She shivered. Just the rumble of his deep voice had awakened an ache deep inside her, in places she'd never felt ache with such need before.

But they would've been a horrible match. He was so deliciously handsome, with every woman in the room vying for his attention, and she was the plain little mouse nobody ever really noticed. At least not anyone her brother deemed rich enough to put an adequate amount of gold in his pocket.

Aila's throat tightened. How many times had Fergus complained because he hadn't been able to find a suitable mate for her who'd also be advantageous to him? At the ripe old age of twenty-two, it wasn't likely he ever would. After all, a high-born virgin was only worth something if she was still young enough to give the man sons.

In some ways, Fergus had probably been relieved when King Charles mandated this union. Even though it was to his enemy and he wouldn't be making any profit off the deal, at least he'd be rid of her.

She knew she was no prize.

Her hair was too red and unruly, and her eyes too big and set too wide apart. Her chin too prominent and her mouth too thin. Her body too slim, her limbs too short, and her breasts too small. Not to mention the fact she had a willful mouth about her and tended to be disobedient at times.

Highland women should be sturdy in order to bear their husbands many strong sons. Highland women should be robust and tough in order to work from dawn till dusk. Highland women should be soft where it counted, plush, big breasted, and long legged in order for their men to find them attractive enough to bed. And highland women should know their place and speak only when spoken to.

At least that's what her brother Fergus had told her.

If what she'd glimpsed in the shadows of the castle walls between other couples was any indication, the most successful women were exactly like that.

But not her. She was not the sort to be turning any man's head.

It wasn't as if she had no worth whatsoever, though, for she did. Or at least she did when she was allowed to use her skills, which wasn't as often as she liked. Even as a young lass, she'd been fascinated with all manner of herbs and plants and what they could do. When old Margot, the village healer, had offered to teach her, Aila had bubbled over with joy. But that was before Fergus had found out.

The sister of the laird was not supposed to dirty her hands caring for the poor. And the sister of the laird was not supposed to be witness to that which might prove to be unpleasant, like sickness, hunger, poverty, and death. The sister of the laird certainly wasn't supposed to question her brother as to how he cared for his people or chastise him in front of others. The sister of the laird was simply supposed to sit quietly before the fire in her solar and stitch useless patterns upon useless pieces of cloth while waiting for her brother to choose her a husband.

She hadn't been content to do so, however. She'd gone when and where she was needed, even if it had meant defying him and sneaking out of the castle. Even if it had meant being locked in her room for days upon end when caught. But he hadn't broken her spirit. Even when he'd told her he was marrying her off to a Mackay, she'd refused to let him see her distress.

Well, wouldn't her brother be surprised when that marriage didn't happen this morning? He may very well hate the Mackays, but Aila was pretty sure Fergus Gordon, Laird of Castle Skelbo and right hand to the Earl of Sutherland hated her even more.

But then he always had, hadn't he?

Fergus blamed her when he lost his mother the day she'd been born, and then again when their father died not long after at the hands of a stinking Mackay. He'd blamed her for the responsibility of a baby sister and a lairdship being thrust upon him at the tender age of thirteen. For the winters if they were too long and cold, the crops if they weren't bountiful, and any sickness that befell his people. Even though he'd always brought her back token gifts from wherever he traveled, in truth, she was pretty sure he blamed her for having the audacity to breathe the same air he did.

The door to her room suddenly swung open and in rushed Fergus's wife Rhona. "Get yer wee arse outta bed, lass. Daylight be a wasting, and ye have a wedding ta attend, don't ye ken?"

She couldn't help but smile. For as mean as Fergus was, his wife Rhona was just the opposite. From the moment she'd exchanged vows with Aila's brother, Rhona had become the sister she'd always hoped for.

"I thought I'd sleep in a while," Aila teased.

She didn't think it wise to inform Rhona that no wedding would be taking place today. As soon as the Mackay men checked on their laird, the whole castle would know.

"Phish," Rhona laughed. "The Mackay is this very moment waiting for ye at the chapel door. And yer brither sent me ta see what's keeping ye."

Chapter Three

Thank God for men who didn't ask a bunch of stupid questions.

When his two clansmen had entered Ian's room earlier that morning, they hadn't said a word other than to remark on the amount of whisky he'd consumed the night before. And then they'd simply laughed, pleated a clean kilt, dressed him as if he were a baby and they were used to doing so, slapped him on the back, and handed him the biggest damn sword he'd ever seen before shooing him out the door. They'd called it his claymore.

Now he stood at the entrance to the chapel and did his best not to make eye contact with anyone, especially Fergus Gordon, the brother of the complete stranger he was about to take as his wife. For the last thing he needed was for his enemy to discover he wasn't the same Ian Mackay the man had sat down with, face to face, only the evening before.

He had no idea what would happen if he was found out. One thing was for certain, he didn't want to chance it either. If there was one thing he did know about 1643 anywhere, let alone 1643 Scotland, it was that these people were crazy superstitious and incredibly violent. Many a man, and even more than a few women, had without a doubt been burned at the stake for much lesser crimes than possessing some dead guy's body.

He still couldn't believe it. Not the truck accident, not the dying, not Fate, not his promise, and certainly not being transported almost four hundred years into the past. And that was even after he'd spent the night doing exactly what Fate had suggested. He'd concentrated on the other Ian Mackay's memories. But even now with all those life experiences firmly ingrained, it still didn't seem real.

Still, he had made some progress. He could now competently speak and understand the nuances of the Gaelic language, so that was no longer a problem. And yes, he even kind of recognized the two Mackay men who'd helped him dress this morning. Their names were Shamus and Hamish. He even remembered the other Ian's uncle, the clan chieftain Laird William Mackay, who'd sent him here, and he could even recite their last conversation verbatim if asked of him. What he couldn't understand was why this Ian Mackay had been chosen for this particular task in the first place.

The only conclusion he could come to was that it had been expected he'd fail.

Most of the other Ian's memories revolved around drinking, whoring, and fighting. Those that didn't directly involve drinking, whoring, and fighting were centered on someone else drinking, whoring, and fighting.

The man was a mess.

He had no real skills, no education, and no desire to better himself in any way, let alone any sense of what responsibility meant.

In other words, the original Ian Mackay of 1643 Scotland was an absolute, fucking idiot.

Perhaps that was why he'd been chosen for this job

in the first place. After all, anybody with two brain cells to rub together would've run the other direction as fast as their highlander legs could've carried them. But not the Ian Mackay of 1643. He was being tasked with marrying his clan's enemy's sister and hadn't so much as blinked an eye at the suggestion.

He hadn't even cared if Fergus Gordon and The Earl of Sutherland didn't like the arrangement? They certainly couldn't just kill him outright without garnering unwanted notice. They wouldn't even be able to object out loud to the union without angering and disobeying the king. Even though the Mackay chieftain had promised him a lairdship and a small castle of his own if he did go through with the marriage, the original Ian would've gladly done it for free just to fuck with the other clan.

But if left up to that Ian Mackay, the man would've failed. Chieftain William Mackay wouldn't have had to give up anything.

This Ian Mackay, however, had no intentions of failing. Too much was riding on this deal. If he succeeded, Fate had promised him a chance to go back and save the men he'd lost. Oh no, he wouldn't fail, not even if the Gordon woman was a hideous troll like her brother.

Not that she was, or at least he hoped she wasn't.

It was weird. He could remember what the other Ian had eaten last night for dinner. He could even remember almost every drink the man had taken. He certainly remembered the sassy little serving wench who'd sat on his lap and wiggled her sweet ass against Ian Mackay's groin. But for the life of him, he couldn't remember one single feature of the woman he was supposed to marry this morning, not even her name. That did worry him.

All the Gordon women he'd seen so far had been a little scary looking. Not that they were ugly, because they weren't. It was that they all looked like they could take him with one hand tied behind their backs and without breaking a sweat. That was taking in consideration that this Ian Mackay was no small man. He was well over six feet if he were an inch and a brawny son-of-a-bitch to boot.

The women of this clan were all probably less than a head shorter than him, almost as broad shouldered, and thick armed with huge ugly-ass feet. Their breasts, oh my God, their breasts. Not that he didn't appreciate a nice rack as much as the next guy, but theirs were all at least a triple D if there was such a thing. A man could suffocate between those boobs and not be found for a week if he wasn't careful.

A sudden draft of chilly air had him anchoring the blue and green wool plaid of his kilt down about his knees, and his face went warm. Of all the things he'd never considered in his life, what a highlander wore beneath his garb was probably close to the top of his list. It was nothing, absolutely nothing. His ass and other parts were as bare as the day the original Ian Mackay had been born with them. And those other parts?

Ian smiled for the first time all morning. Not that in his old life his genitals had been inadequate, for they had been very nice. But this one, this particular package was downright exceptional. This cock was at least a full inch longer than his old one, and its girth was no laughing matter either.

Not that he'd spent an enormous amount of time checking out his new body in that damned cold loch, but he had had to wash it clean of all that vomit and god knew what else. And anyway, wasn't it second nature to take stock of what he now had to work with?

He almost giggled like a school girl. Being sent almost four hundred years into the past might be a frigging nightmare, but at least he'd gotten a more than decent cock out of the deal. He would've been damn pissed if he'd awoken with a skinny, little pencil dick.

****

It wasn't possible. The man couldn't be alive. He simply couldn't be.

Aila starred at her reflection and shook her head. How could she have been so wrong? It's not as if she hadn't seen her share of dead bodies over the years, because she certainly had. She could've sworn that Ian Mackay was without a doubt dead as dead could be when she'd walked into his room last evening. He hadn't been moving or breathing, and his skin was already cool to the touch. Not to mention the fact he'd been a little on the stiff side. So how then could that same man be very much alive this morning and waiting for her at the chapel? It didn't make sense.

She shivered. Perhaps he wasn't even a flesh and blood man anymore. Perhaps Ian Mackay had been the victim of a fairy kidnapping in the middle of the night and was now a man who was neither dead nor alive but simply a creature of the shadows, a *sidhe*, an *Aos Si*.

She'd heard stories about them all her life.

Guilt filled her. If Ian Mackay was a *sidhe* now, it was all her fault. She should've alerted his men and her brother to the fact he was dead when she first found him. She kenned their customs verra well, and she'd broken them. Someone should've sat with his lifeless body, so it wasn't left alone for even a moment. It should've been prepared and anointed with protective charms so the fairies couldn't get to him.

Yes, it was her fault, completely and totally.

And now she was going to have to pay a horrible price for her mistake of the night before.

But how could she possibly go through with marrying such a being?

She couldn't.

But then again, there was no way Fergus would listen to anything she had to say this morning. And if she did try to tell him what she'd seen the night before, he certainly wouldn't be willing to go against the dictates of King Charles and stop the wedding, especially with the Earl of Sutherland in residence. Oh no, he'd get angry with her, very angry.

Then what was she going to do?

Aila searched her mind. There had to be something. Then it came to her. She needed to make a quick detour on her way to the chapel, because if anybody was in need of a protective charm right now, it was her.

Her feet had no sooner hit the last step of the stairs when her sister-in-law waylaid her. "There ye are. Hurry along now. Yer brither, yer guests, and yer groom are all waiting, ye ken?"

Aila tried to stall. She needed to get to the kitchen. All she needed was a simple hunk of bread, because everyone knew that before going out where fairies might be congregating, it was customary to put bread in one's pocket for protection. Bread meant hearth and home, a symbol of life, and thereby disliked by fairies and their captives. So bread it had to be. But first she needed to get past Rhona.

"Go on ahead," Aila said. "I'll be right along. I'm just going ta grab a quick bite. Just a crust of bread, ye ken. I'm near famished."

Rhona laughed, linked arms with her, and started pulling her toward the door. Dread filled Aila.

"That's what ye get for sleeping half the morning away." Her sister-in-law laughed once more. "Ye've waited this long ta break yer fast, ye can wait a bit longer. After the ceremony, yer brither has a wedding feast planned."

Aila quickly sidestepped her. "Just one small crust of bread. It'll only take a second. I promise."

She could hear Rhona's sigh as she hurried down the hall.

"One crust," her sister-in-law yelled. "I'll nae have Fergus telling me I'm far too lenient with ye again. It's much too important a day for the Sutherland clan ta be making yer brither and laird angry."

As quickly as she could, Aila made her way to the kitchen, snatched up a chunk of bread, balled it up, and shoved it deep into her pocket. Now she was as ready to face the *sidhe* who was about to become her husband as she would ever be.

With a grimace, she returned to the great hall and allowed Rhona to tug her the rest of the way through the castle door.

"Now come along," her sister-in-law said sweetly. "Ye've kept yer groom waiting long enough."

Aila fingered her protection charm of bread through the cloth of her skirt, gulped, and followed.

****

Wow! Holy Mother of God!

Ian's breath caught, and his heart pounded hard in his chest at the sight of the little redhead walking toward him. She was beyond lovely. She was stunning. Her body was lithe and compact in the golden dress she wore, draped in Mackay plaid. Just the right size to tuck under an arm and up against his heart. And her breasts... Oh my God, her breasts were perfect. Nothing like the other women of her clan, hers were more the size of ripe cantaloupes instead of watermelons. Large enough to nip and suck and play with, without the worry of falling in and suffocation. Her lush lips, wide open inquisitive eyes, dimpled chin... And her slender waist, not to mention those long legs and tiny little feet with what looked to be ten perfect little toes peeking out...

Yes, this had to be her. God, please let it be her.

She simply had to be Fergus Gordon's sister. Thank god, she didn't in any way physically resemble her fiercely hard highlander brother. There was an air of that same stubborn confidence about her, though. A very attractive air to be sure. Ian had always appreciated a strong-willed woman.

Even if he hadn't been staring in her direction, his heart would've still leapt half out of his chest the moment she walked through those castle doors and straight toward him. There was just something about her that called to his soul. An overpowering feeling of rightness, of family, of providence, of finally coming home after being away for ever so long. A feeling he hadn't realized had been missing from his life since he'd returned from Afghanistan. It was like a bright light being suddenly turned on in the middle of a dark-as-night room and like the warmth flooding a space that had been previously cold as death itself.

A part of him wanted to rush to her, but an even greater part wanted to run away as fast and as far as he could get. This wasn't fair to her. She wasn't going to get the man she thought she was marrying. She wasn't even going to get a man capable of loving anyone anymore. All she was going to get was an empty shell and what was left of a scarred mind.

Instead of running though, he willed himself to stand completely still and wait. He couldn't afford for her, or her brother, to become suspicious. In order for any of this to work, he had to be the epitome of the original Ian Mackay and act like a man being forced to marry the sister of his enemy. Too many eyes were upon him this day, and there was too much to lose. He had to do this for his squad. He had to make his mistakes right, and this was his only chance to do that. But God help the poor girl for being unlucky enough to be the one about to be stuck with him.

Not for the first time since waking in another man's body in the Scottish highlands and in the year 1643, Ian Mackay wished desperately for a drink, or two, or five, along with an Ativan or a Valium to steady his nerves.

Then, right there on the steps leading into the small church, the priest joined their hands with a strip of Mackay plaid. Ian's world tilted upon its axis, and for a moment, he forgot to breath. This was happening. It was really happening. He was in a stranger's body in a strange country in an even stranger time about to marry a complete stranger. Could he really do this to her?

Warmth from her small bare fingers spread across his palm, up his arm, and around his neck before

33

settling square in his chest. She felt it, too. He knew she did. He could tell by the way she suddenly trembled, by the way her breathing quickened, her graceful nostrils flared, and the pupils of her deep green eyes dilated.

Then the priest looped the strip of plaid up and over their joined wrists a second time. "Do ye, Ian, and ye, Aila, consent ta live tagether for the rest of yer lives in accordance ta God's will?"

Ian wanted to answer, really he did, but in the end, the only noise he managed to get past his lips was a grunt as he nodded his head.

Aila, though, her voice was clear as a bell and as lovely as a song when she said, "Aye."

What a pretty name. Aila. It fit her. It was small. It was lovely.

The priest looped the end of the swatch of plaid about their wrists for a third time. "Will ye share each other's pain and burdens and laughter and tears as ye travel through this life?"

Again, Ian nodded, no longer trusting himself to even try and speak.

Just as before, Aila said, "Aye," loudly and clearly.

Once again, the priest looped the fabric about their wrists, but this time he tied the two ends into a secure knot. "As much as Ian and Aila have consented ta be joined in marriage before God and these witnesses, it is the decree of the Church that their lives be long, their loins fruitful, and their days be filled with plenty."

He turned in a circle with his arms stretched wide before once more facing Ian and Aila. "May the elements be always with ye. From the East, may the air breath inta ye a purity of heart along with the rising of the sun each new day. May the South, with its fire, fill ye with passion even during the darkest of winter nights. May the water from the West give ye peace even in times of great sorrow. And from the North and its element of earth, may yer lands feed ye and yer people, and may ye always prosper."

And with that, Ian Mackay, former staff sergeant from almost four hundred years in the future and from itty-bitty Johnsville, Ohio, was now a married laird in the 1643 highlands of Scotland.

Chapter Four

She'd done it. She'd actually really gone and done it. She'd married herself to a fey creature, a *sidhe*, a monster, and all because her brother and her king had expected it of her.

Aila sat between her new husband and her brother, chewing her lip, and trying to decide which one of them she was more afraid of.

Fergus was in a black mood today to be sure. He glared at anyone who dared look his direction, and if the level of the whisky in his tankard was any indication, he was well into his cups and it was still midmorning. He hadn't liked being told he'd give his sister to his enemy and not get anything in return, and she knew it. But he'd obeyed the king's dictate all the same.

And then there was her new husband.

Ian Mackay sat staring straight ahead as if he desperately wanted to leap up and make a mad dash for the castle door. It was probably the bread. Her protection charm was no doubt making the *sidhe* uncomfortable.

And a *sidhe* he definitely was.

From a distance, she'd watched the real Ian Mackay the night before as he drank with her brother, and she'd observed the subtle nuances of the man. The way he'd moved his hands incessantly while talking, the way he'd laughed very loud at anything and everything being said, and the way his eyes had followed other women around the great hall, like a wolf stalking its next meal. Oh yes, she'd definitely watched him. She'd wanted to garner all the information she could about the man who'd become her husband today, and she had not liked a single thing she'd seen except for his features.

This Ian Mackay, he was different in every way except those marvelous features. This Ian didn't use his hands to gesture when he spoke at all, and this Ian hadn't laughed once, not even quietly, since she'd been in his presence. This Ian hadn't downed a single tankard of ale as of yet. This Ian Mackay had not so much as glanced at any other women, not even Izzy, the serving lass who'd spent half the previous evening securely upon his lap.

No, this Ian and the man of last evening were nothing alike. It was the oddest feeling to look into those same stormy blue eyes and see a completely different person staring back at her. Not to mention she'd seen the man stone cold dead upon his floor, face down in a pool of vomit only a few hours ago.

He really was a *sidhe*.

That was the only explanation that made any sense.

She fingered the hunk of bread in her pocket, glad for its protection, and searched her mind for what to do next. One couldn't really be a wife to someone possessed by fairies, could one? And even if one could, no one with half a brain would want to be. What if the fairies decided that, since she was now this Ian Mackay's wife, she belonged to them, too?

She shuddered. Could this day get any worse?

Fergus's sudden bellow snapped her out of her introspection. "A wedding dance with yer laird and brither, dear sister," he slurred.

She didn't want to. But at the same time, she knew it could prove to be even more dangerous to refuse. Everyone who knew him knew Fergus Gordon did not like being refused anything. If anyone dared, there was always a price to pay.

She didn't want him to dance with her today of all days. Over the years, they'd shared a dance when given no other choice, and she didn't wish to mar one of the very few pleasant memories she had of her brother. But this day, this dance would be anything but pleasant and she knew it, for Fergus's anger emanated from him like the sheen of sweat upon his brow.

She looked toward Ian, but her *sidhe* of a husband was no help at all. He was still staring straight ahead, not saying a word, not drinking his ale, not gesturing with his hands, not following the movements of the other women in the room, and most certainly not laughing.

So slowly she rose. "Aye, of course. I'd be honored."

The moment she was within her brother's arms, Aila knew it was an even bigger mistake than she'd thought.

He drew her in close and whispered in her ear. "Ye'll no be dirtying good Gordon blood with a filthy Mackay spawn, do ye ken? I know ye ken how ta prevent a babe being made. I've heard the women speak of it. And if ye ken what's good for ye, ye'd better be doing as I say. I may have been forced ta marry ye off ta me enemy, but that does nae mean I give ye permission ta give him bairns."

Tears stung her eyes as he twirled her around before bringing back in close. "Let this be a warning. Do nae go against me on this, sister. For if ye dare birth even a single Mackay bastard, I'll make sure it never draws a breath right before ye draw yer last. Do we understand each other?"

If there was one thing she knew about *sidhes*, it was that once a man was taken over by the fairies, he could no longer father children. It was a well-known fact. So Aila simply nodded.

Fergus laughed as he released her so quickly she almost lost her balance. "Mackay," he once more bellowed. "I've done all I can do and now 'tis up ta ye. I've welcomed ye into my home without slitting yer throat, I've given ye me sister as wife as our king commanded, and I've allowed ye the use of my favorite priest ta make it binding and legal. Now 'tis time for ye ta do yer part."

He pushed her toward the table, and this time she did stumble. "Come and collect the lass. Take her ta the room I so graciously provided and fuck her till she bleeds. Then I want ye both outta me castle and off me land. And ye best hope I nae ever have reason ta lay eyes on either of ye again. For next time, ye won't find me ta be quite so hospitable like."

****

Fergus Gordon was an absolute prick.

Ian watched his new bride pace the small space of the room he'd been given and wanted nothing more than to march back down the stairs and punch her bastard of a brother right in the nose. How in the hell was he going to get her calm enough now to do what

39

they both had no choice but to do?

"Are you hungry?" he asked.

She pulled a chunk of brown something from her pocket and held it out before her and shook her head. "Nae. Bread. I have bread, ye ken?"

He motioned to the tankard of ale he'd brought up with him. "Thirsty then?"

Again, she simply shook her head no.

From his predecessor's memories, Ian knew full well what was expected of them both. Not only expected but demanded. In the eyes of the Church and the law in 1643 Scotland, he and Aila weren't married until he'd taken her virginity and shown the proof. Obviously, highlanders didn't have the time or the patience to slowly woo their love interest.

Oh no, they were all a bunch of barbarians of the highest order. But thank God, they weren't demanding to watch, which they certainly could have. At least he didn't have to worry about preforming before an audience. That was, as long as he got this over with quickly before they came looking to see what was taking so long.

He motioned toward the bed. "Would you, I mean, would ye like to get comfortable?"

Again, she shook her head and this time backed up a step. "I'm nae tired. 'Tis barely mid-day."

He couldn't do this. He wasn't a barbarian like they were and couldn't be. Even if it meant his squad had to stay dead for an eternity or more. He simply hadn't been raised thinking it was all right to force himself upon another person, even if that person was his wife. *Especially* if that person was his wife. The thought of simply bending the lovely little Aila over the bed and getting the job done and over with quickly was making him both sick to his stomach and hard as a rock.

No, no, no, no, no. He wouldn't listen to this cock. Even if his old one had been attention deprived for a very long time.

Not only would such a blatant act of disrespect break his mother's heart if she knew what he'd just been contemplating, but if his father had even an inkling, he'd have had him out in the woodshed so fast Ian wouldn't have known what had hit him.

Women were to be respected.

Women were to be cherished.

Women were to be loved and protected.

It was a husband's duty to care for his wife in all things. And hers to care for him. And duty was something Ian understood. He could no more force his new bride to do anything she didn't wish to do, than he could strike her. It wasn't how real men behaved and certainly not how midwest farmer's sons or even piss-poor staff sergeants acted, as far as that was concerned.

He took a deep breath and tried again. "Perhaps if we lie down together and just talk. You, I mean ye and I are man and wife and have a need to get to intimately know each other."

Aila held her chunk of bread out in front of herself as if the thing could protect her from him and backed up until she was flush against the wall. "Ye are a Mackay, and an unnatural one at that. I need know nae more."

Fuck, fuck, fuck, fuck, fuck, fuck.

So, what now? He needed a plan.

How was he going to coax his new bride into bed? Seduction was always an option. That was if he could get her close enough to cooperate. She simply had to be scared. After all, she was without a doubt an innocent, and he was still very much an enemy of her clan from the sounds of her brother.

Ian almost laughed. Seduction. Who was he fooling? The entire extent of his sexual experiences with women consisted of two quick trysts before he'd gone into the service and not much more than paid professionals since he'd been out. Prostitutes didn't ask questions, and they sure as hell didn't expect long-term romances, promises, loyalty, or love. At the time, and with his issues and limitations, sex for pay had made his love life a hell of a lot easier.

But the young woman standing before him right now wasn't a prostitute. She was his wife. So how was he going to convince her to willingly climb in his bed?

He almost chuckled out loud as he remembered a training exercise he'd once been a part of. Perhaps he wasn't seduction savvy, but that didn't mean he was without any knowledge of basic human behavior either. Not that wives and war-time combatants had much in common, but then a battle was a battle, wasn't it?

Rule number one: Attempt to gain your opponent's trust.

Ian smiled at Aila and shrugged. "You're right about one thing. I am a Mackay, but as my lawful wife, so are ye now. As my wife, I'll never hurt you, I promise. You can trust me."

Then he made a production of walking over to the fireplace, turning his back to her, and stoking the embers until the flames leapt and the wood crackled.

She scoffed. "I'll nae be trusting the likes of ye any time soon. I ken what ye are. I know ye ta be a *sidhe*, and do nae be trying ta deny it."

He turned back around toward her. "What the hell's a *sidhe*?"

But before the words were even completely out of his mouth, the original Ian Mackay's memories gave him the answer he was searching for. A fairy, a *sidhe* was a fae creature, and not a very nice one.

Really? His wife thought him to be some kind of frigging-ass fairy? The Scots were a superstitious lot, but this fairy shit was ridiculous. It was on the tip of his tongue to tell her so when, from the serious look on her face, he knew she'd meant exactly what she'd said.

She put her hands on her hips and glared at him. "Aye, ye are a *sidhe*. And before ye say another word, I realize it's partially my fault. I should've told yer men or at least me brither when I found ye dead on the floor of this very room last night, but I did nae. And I admit, even I was nae certain the fairies had possessed ye until after the wedding."

She held the chunk of bread she'd been clutching since entering the room at arm's length. "After I saw how ye could nae sit still with me protection charm anywhere near ye and how ye do nae act or laugh or even talk the way Ian Mackay did before I found him dead, then I knew. Aye, ye are nae truly Ian Mackay but a *sidhe* for sure. So ye must leave here without me and go back to ye own, 'cause I'll nae be going anywhere with ye."

Ian shook his head. Damn, how was he going to explain this away? Fuck Tobias Moiré, or Fate, or whatever the little creep wanted to call himself, for not telling him Aila had seen the original Ian Mackay dead. That little tidbit of information would've certainly

43

come in handy.

Instead of saying what he was thinking, he sighed. So much for rule number one, and time to move on.

Number 2: If you fail to earn your enemies' trust, then try using the art of distraction and throw them off guard.

He strode to where she stood and snatched the chunk of bread from her hand. He took a big bite, chewed and swallowed, before handing her back the remainder. "If I were a *sidhe*, do you think I could eat your, um, protection charm without it doing any damage to me?"

Her eyes became big as saucers, and her mouth gaped open. "I—I—I do nae ken. Ye are the first *sidhe* I've ever met face to face."

Ian took a deep breath as he moved in closer until they were nose to nose. "If I were a *sidhe*, would I do this?" He kissed her.

The moment their lips touched, he knew what his next step would be. Excitement like he'd never known skittered along his spine as his cock roared to life. His blood-starved brain completely forgot whatever he'd been thinking, and nothing mattered except keeping her mouth upon his.

Soft, her lips were so soft and full and luscious. She tasted of springtime, warm and fresh, with just a hint of that damn bread and a touch of ale. He wanted to drink her in, sate his thirst. At the same time, he wanted to toss her on the bed and delve deep into all the other hidden wonders he had no doubt she possessed. He was in the process of wrapping his arms around her and doing just that when she spoke without even breaking their kiss.

"Aye," she sighed, her breath mingling with his own. "A *sidhe* would certainly do that, I'd think. They are a tricky bunch."

He chuckled. He couldn't help himself. But he also decided it was time to employ rule number three. A rule that had served him well over the years.

Number 3: If you are having difficulty throwing your opponent off guard, overwhelm their senses until they concede defeat.

"I am not a *sidhe*, but simply a man, Aila," he whispered as he nibbled the tender skin of her neck. "Your man, your husband to be exact. I don't know what you think you saw last night, perhaps you were simply sleepwalking, but I'm very much alive and well and quite capable of making you a very happy woman if only you'll allow it."

She shivered in his arms. "I'd expect a *sidhe* ta say as much."

He chuckled again as his hand found a breast. He kneaded the perky globe of flesh and tweaked a taunt nipple.

She sighed, and her warm breath against his neck once more sent shivers of lust skittering down his spine. That was until she pushed out of his arms. "There is nae ye can do to convince me ye are nae a *sidhe* now instead of a warm-blooded man, Ian Mackay. For only a fae creature such as yerself could do such magic with just the touch of a hand or lips."

He shook his head. So much for overwhelming her senses. It was definitely time for rule number four.

Number 4: If rules number one, two, and three don't work as you'd like, then throw the damn rule book right out the window and follow your own instincts.

"So, you're saying these fae creatures aren't warm-blooded, Aila?" He already knew the answer. Ian Mackay's memories had nicely filled in more details than he ever wanted to know about the *sidhe* and the fairies and even the stupid bogy-man.

He pulled her back into his embrace, and she snuggled in closer as he tightened his arms about her.

"Nae," she whispered. "Ye ken they aren't. Everyone kens a *sidhe* is as cold as death inside."

He grasped her small hand within his own and guided it down the length of his body then wrapped her fingers around the outline of his hard, hot cock. "Does this convince ye I'm not a *sidhe*?"

Once more, Ian took her mouth in a deep kiss, but this time he lifted her into his arms and strolled toward the bed. To his surprise, Aila didn't have another single word to say.

Chapter Five

Ian's hot mouth came down over her bare nipple once more, and Aila moaned as she arched her back, begging him without words to stay right where he was and keep doing exactly what he was doing. Time had lost all meaning long ago. They could've been in this bed for mere moments or days, and she wouldn't have known the difference. For if time was counted by kisses instead of grains of sand shifting through an hourglass, then they'd been here an eternity already. A glorious eternity, filled with pure sensation. She was drunk with it.

Excitement spread to places Aila had forgotten she even had, and for the first time in her life, she understood the secretive little smiles the common women around her had passed back and forth between themselves after their quick trysts with the castles highlanders in one dark corner or another. If it had been this way with all of them, then she'd definitely been missing out on something momentous.

His mouth suddenly traveled across her ribcage and down her abdomen, and she forgot to breathe. God his tongue was a magnificent thing. It swirled upon and sucked at her skin. It delved into her belly button and back out again. It licked and teased as his teeth nipped their way farther down her body.

Of their own volition, her hands fisted in his hair,

his silky midnight black hair, and she wasn't sure if her intention was to push his mouth even lower or simply hold on to him for dear life, and she didn't care. The only thing important right now was that what he was doing, and how he was making her feel, didn't end.

Not yet.

God, please not yet.

The place between her thighs, the place she'd always dared not touch, throbbed in a rhythm that matched perfectly the pounding of her heart. There was something she needed, something that would ease the ache, and she knew it, could feel it. But she couldn't grasp what that was. All she was sure of was, whatever it was she needed, Ian Mackay held the power to provide.

Yes, she'd seen people coupling from time to time. One couldn't live in a castle with so many others and not be witness to intimate goings on occasionally. But this was different. Perhaps because her new husband was a *sidhe* and thereby a magical creature with magical abilities. But what he was doing now, how he was touching and tasting her was so far beyond merely intimate, it was mind-boggling, and earth-shattering, and life-altering.

And just when she thought it couldn't possibly get better, it did.

Ian slid farther down until his chin rested right on her most private parts. His breath sent whispers of warm air through the curls there, causing the throbbing to intensify to a wonderfully painful level.

He parted her with his fingers and blew a puff of air right on her core. She almost came up off the bed.

"Ah, look at what a pretty little thing I've found,"

he chuckled.

Heat infused her cheeks with the knowledge that he was looking at a part of her body she herself hadn't had the courage to explore. And pretty? What did he mean by pretty? Aila knew for a fact there was nothing bonny about any part of her. The man really was a devil, a *sidhe*, someone nae ta be trusted if he was saying such things.

She squirmed in an attempt to get away, but his arms didn't allow her to move very far.

He looked her right in the eye. "Too much too fast?"

She gulped and nodded, and then shook her head. "I do nae ken," she finally cried. "I'm just...I feel...I need...I..." She sighed and gave up trying to explain and lay back. She didn't have the words to make him understand what was going on inside her. Especially when she didn't understand herself.

Ever so slowly he began again, and Aila was tempted to laugh at first as his tongue lashed out licking the inside of her thighs. But by the time he reached her knees, she was no longer laughing, but panting, and before he made it to her shins, the throbbing she'd put out of her mind only moments before was back in full force.

Then he kissed her ankles and slid his tongue along the instep of her foot. First the right, and then the left.

It was like being struck by lightning.

Shivers of hot delight rushed straight up both legs exploding outward as they reached her core until she shattered into a million tiny pieces.

Over and over her body spasmed in ecstasy where only moments before she'd throbbed with need. Only after the last spasm faded away, did Aila realize that Ian was no longer still down at her feet, but right beside her, rocking her gently as the pieces of her soul found their way back together again.

With a smile on her face, she closed her eyes and snuggled into his embrace. Perhaps being married to a *sidhe* wasn't such a horrible thing after all, especially if his magical touch brought about more glorious tremors like the one she'd just had.

"Aila?"

She opened her eyes and stared into the oh-so handsome face staring back at her. It really was a shame he was a *sidhe* and no longer a real-life flesh and blood man. She'd never get the chance to know the real Ian Mackay, and that saddened her. But there wasn't time to contemplate one Ian Mackay as opposed to another right now, for this Ian Mackay was looking at her as if he were confused about something.

"Aye?" she whispered.

"We're not quite done," he managed to squeak out. "You do realize that, don't you?"

For a moment, she was confused, and then it dawned on her. Of course, the rutting part. Heat wicked up her face, and her breath caught in her chest. How could she have forgotten about the rutting part?

She'd always found the sight of the actual copulation a mixture of disturbing and exciting. All those grunts and groans and moans she'd ardently listened to. All those dark corner trysts she wasn't supposed to watch but did. Naked bodies touching so close that parts of one actually joined with parts of the other.

The throbbing that had subsided started up once

more. "Aye," she whispered again. "I suppose we had better be at it then."

He rolled on top of her, spreading her legs, and positioning himself between them. "The first time hurts a little, but after that it'll be okay, I promise." He nudged himself forward just an inch.

Aila shook her head. She knew exactly what was poking at her, and it was going to hurt a lot more than a little to get that huge thing where he was trying to put it. She'd gauged the difference in the size of his live cock as opposed to his dead one when he placed her hand over it earlier, but with all of the wonderful things he'd done to her only moments before, she'd forgotten how shocked she'd been at its growth.

"I'm sorry ta be telling ye this now," she gasped. "Especially since I just said we'd better be at it, but that thing is nae gonna fit. Ye are too big."

Stormy blue eyes stared down at her with understanding as midnight black strands of his hair kissed her cheeks. "It'll fit. You'll stretch to accommodate it. Trust me. That's how this thing works and has been working since the beginning of time."

Then he pressed against her opening again, the very tip burrowing between her curls and caressing the place no man had ever touched before.

"Nae," she squealed. "I'm telling ye. Ye are too big. It's nae like I have nae seen more than a few man parts in my time ta know the difference. I live in a castle with hundreds of men coming and going every day, and there's nae way ta avoid seeing things ye wish ye had nae seen. But I've nae ever in me life laid eyes on one as big as yours. It's nae natural I'm telling ye, and it's nae gonna fit."

****

For a moment, Ian rested his forehead on Aila's, slowly breathing in and out her essence and trying to think of a way to convince his new bride he wouldn't cause her permanent damage with his cock. Or at least with what was now his cock.

God, this was harder than it should be, and the whole reason he'd avoided virgins for years and years and years. They were always more trouble than they were worth. And even though he was frustrated with her, he still couldn't stop himself from smiling.

A virgin Aila might very well be, but she'd surprised the hell out of him just the same. The woman had orgasmed when he'd done no more than lick her instep. Now that was a woman whose feet he could literally worship at.

While most men were either breast, ass, or leg men, he'd always had a thing for a nicely turned ankle, shapely toes, or a pretty instep. Though he'd never tell a soul, there'd been times when he was a much younger man, he'd jacked off to a Saint Laurent, Prada, or Dolce & Gabbana model in high heels instead of a butt naked playboy bunny. So Aila's response to his licking his way up her lovely little foot had almost had him coming before she did.

The problem still remained. Her brother was downstairs waiting to see a fucking sheet with his sister's virginal blood smeared on it. And much too much was riding on the outcome of the next few minutes to even consider stopping now.

So what then?

God, how he wished he had a fat bowl of weed or at least a nice, warm, special brownie to share with her right now to calm both their nerves. But he didn't. And he didn't have a clue as to whether pot was even grown in 1643 Scotland or who to ask. So along with his previous wish for Ativan or Valium, marijuana was added to his you-are-oh-so-shit-out-of-luck list.

"Are ye asleep," she whispered.

He prodded at her opening with his still rock-hard cock. "Nope, all of me is still very much wide awake."

She had the audacity to squirm and giggle. "Well, get off me then. We both ken its nae gonna work, and ye are near ta mashing me flat, *sidhe*."

Instead of doing what she asked or again arguing the fact he wasn't some kind of magical fairy creature, he slid back down her body until his chin once more rested upon the top of her pussy. If just licking her instep had given her an orgasm, then his tongue all over her clit was bound to make her oblivious to the fact he was about to take her virginity. If not, it was well worth the try.

He blew on curls the same vibrant shade of red as the hair upon her head and smiled as Aila shivered. He flicked out his tongue and tickled the nub hidden there, and she moaned deep and long. The sound so excited him, a drop of pre-cum leaked from his cock to wet the sheets. He ignored it, too wrapped up in the prize set before him.

She tasted of wild honeysuckle and cranberries of all things. All warm and sweet and welcoming, with just a hint of tart. The combination fit her, and it brought a smile to his face as he delved in once again, this time licking harder and faster and deeper.

Aila's next moan was much longer than the one before it and ended in a quick little pant. Oh yes, before he was done, she was definitely going to forget to be worried about the size of his dick.

Her hands fisted in his hair as he latched onto her clit with a vengeance and sucked. Over and over, he lathed her hard, little nub with his tongue as she bucked and moaned and shuddered beneath him. But he wasn't done teasing her yet, and instead inserted first one finger and then another deep into her hot, wet pussy.

This time, with a gasp, the moans turned into all out pants.

Ian's balls churned with need, and his dick pulsed to the rapid rhythm of her heartbeat.

With each stroke of his tongue, the closer she came to release, but every time those first little telltale shivers raced through her, he backed off until she was writhing with need and begging him to end her suffering. That's when he took pity on her. That's when he slid back up her body. And that's when he thrust past her virginal barrier and seated himself deep within her warmth.

Sweat broke out on his forehead from the strain of holding back. And though he longed to pound into her furiously, he held perfectly still and waited for her to adjust.

Slowly, she did.

Where a moment before she still had her fingers tightly entwined in his hair, they now slid leisurely down to grasp his shoulders, her nails ever-so-slightly digging into his flesh. That sensation itself almost had him coming before he'd even completed one stroke.

He took deep breaths and concentrated on the sound of her breathing. She'd made a single small gasp as he first entered her, but now she was softly mewling and beginning to wiggle her sweet ass as she locked her legs around his hips and rocked forward.

That was his cue, and with a soul deep quiver he thrust forward, once then twice, then so furiously he lost count. And Aila met him stroke for stroke. It was glorious. She was glorious, and Ian was so engrossed in what they were doing that he forgot everything except for the feeling of her sweet little pussy wrapped tightly about his cock.

It didn't matter that he was in a strange land and a strange time, let alone in a complete stranger's body. It didn't matter that he'd just become the husband of a woman who was a stranger to him. It didn't even matter that her crazy brother, who was apparently his enemy, was downstairs and could, and probably would, walk in at any minute. All that mattered was being inside Aila, balls deep, to the hilt, and straight through the heart. It was the most wonderful place he could ever remember being.

Time lost all meaning. The only thing that mattered to Ian's lust-filled brain was the need to move even faster. So he did, and so did she, and within moments, they were both shouting their climaxes to the rooftops.

****

Aye, there was no doubt whatsoever, her husband was definitely a *sidhe*. For no real-life flesh and blood man could've done the things he'd done to and with her body, and still be of this world.

Aila glanced Ian's way for at least the tenth time in as many minutes. They'd been riding for three days now, and though there were his two clansmen and their horses between them, the feel of his naked body pressed against hers while they'd slept entwined in his plaid on the ground the night before still hadn't faded.

She sighed.

What a shame that women married to real live highlanders would never know the pleasure she did. Though it probably wasn't the least bit wise to meekly trail a fae creature out of her brother's castle to only god knew where, she did nae care. For right now, *sidhe* or nae, flesh and blood or nae, she'd follow Ian Mackay anywhere he wished to roam. Especially if he continued to work his magic upon her in their bed chamber when they reached their new home. That was, if and when they ever reached their new home.

Her bottom had long ago gone numb while riding from dawn till dusk. She was tired of eating nothing more than tasteless oats, dry bread, and stringy meat. If she had to sleep another night on the cold, hard ground, even while wrapped within the warmth of Ian's arms, she'd probably cry.

But then almost anywhere, even if it was cold or hard had to be better than sleeping another night under her brother's roof, didn't it? Though she already dearly missed his wife Rhona, she hoped Fergus was right and she'd never have reason to lay eyes on him again.

He'd sneered when Ian presented the bloodied sheet, and he tossed it in the fire a heartbeat later, but not before he mocked him for taking so long to get the job done. With his next breath, he had demanded the 'dirty stinking' Mackays, especially her, leave his castle and never return. To make matters worse, every Gordon and Sutherland warrior present in the great hall echoed his sentiment. She was a Mackay now, a sworn enemy. She would've done the same if it had been someone else who married her clan's greatest rival. So she hadn't really expected anything else.

Still, tears stung her eyes. How could her own people treat her so cruelly? The same people she'd cared for all her life. She'd bandaged their wounds, treated their sick, fed their hungry, delivered their bairns, and even given the plaid off her back, on more than one occasion, so others wouldn't feel the bitter cold bite of winter. They could've simply turned their backs and snubbed her. Their thrown sticks and stones and hurtful words had nae been necessary.

But what had she expected? She really and truly was a Mackay now.

No, make that a *dirty-stinking* Mackay and no longer welcome on Gordon or Sutherland lands.

She was an outcast, and all because a king who cared little for Scotland and thought himself a god, had decided her fate.

She glanced at Ian again. What would life among the Mackays and as the laird's wife be like? She hadn't really had much of a chance to ask questions. After riding for hours on end, all any of them had wanted to do at the end of the day was eat quickly and lay their heads down to sleep before beginning the same process come morning.

Still, it bothered her.

Would the Mackay clansmen and clanswomen where they were headed accept her as their lady? And if so, would Ian allow her to treat the sick among them or would he be like Fergus and feel it was not her place? Would she be forced to sneak and do what she needed to behind his back just as she had with her brother?

She hoped not.

And the biggest part of her didn't really believe she would have to.

Ian Mackay wasn't Fergus Gordon. He hadn't once been mean or cruel or vindictive, at least not that she'd seen any signs of. But then he wasn't actually a real highlander like Fergus anymore either, was he? No, he was a *sidhe* and she'd best not forget it. Who other than the gods knew exactly what a *sidhe* could or would be capable of?

Suddenly, he glanced toward her and smiled. "Shamus and Hamish say we're almost to our new home, lass. That means tonight we sleep in a real bed."

Then he winked.

Aila's heart did a little flip-flop in her chest. *Sidhe* or nae, it didn't matter. What mattered was, he was her husband and their life together was about to begin in earnest.

Chapter Six

The very beginning of May 1643
Borve Castle

There was no way in hell this was now or had ever been a fucking castle. There had to have been a misunderstanding between Shamus, Hamish, and the Mackay Chieftain. A mistake that could easily be rectified if he could simply hold his temper long enough.

With a sick feeling in the pit of his stomach, Ian glanced around the pile of mostly ruble and shook his head. "You, I mean ye, can't mean to tell me that this," he spread his arms wide, "is what I was promised? This isn't a castle. It's—it's nothing but a bunch of rocks randomly stacked together. And to boot, you're saying my closest neighbors, other than the villagers, are all Sutherlands who killed the last Mackay laird just for the hell of it?"

Shamus had the decency to at least look guilty as he shuffled his feet and glanced off into the distance.

Hamish didn't appear uncomfortable in the least. As a matter of fact, the other highlander guard who'd accompanied him for every step of this journey cackled with glee and bent over almost double, laughing. "I told old Laird William ye'd nae be happy when ye saw ye fine wedding present." Again, Hamish laughed so long and hard he could hardly draw a breath. "Just ask

Shamus if I didn't. And do ye know what the Mackay said? He said it served ye right ta take over Castle Borve and the wee village over there for nae volunteering ta do what yer clan needed just 'cause it needed doing and nae because ye were being paid ta do it. Ye've always been a greedy young whelp, Ian Mackay. Serves ye right."

Ian wanted to punch Hamish in the nose. His fingers itched with the need to do just that or at least wring his gleeful neck. But Aila was watching, her eyes wide with fear. Worse, what appeared to be about a fifty or so scraggly, half-starved strangers had gathered in groups close by to stare at the newcomers. They had to be the villagers Fate and now Hamish had spoken of, and the last thing Ian needed was to start off on the wrong foot with the same people he'd been sent to help.

Shamus shrugged. "I hate ta admit it, but Hamish's right, lad. That's sure enough what the Mackay said ta both of us. Though I honestly do nae think he ever thought ye'd live long enough ta take possession of Borve. He was almost certain Fergus Gordon would kill ye dead before he'd ever marry his sister off ta any Mackay, let alone the grandson of the man who put a sword through his father's heart. I'm pretty sure these lands were only promised to ye in case Fergus failed ta do the deed right proper. I'm thinking Laird William does nae like ye over much. But then, he did catch ye in the stables tupping his daughter that one time, and her newly betrothed ta another. Shame on ye, lad. Shame on ye."

Well, fuck. What was he going to do now?

The tension around him was so thick he could've cut it with a knife. The town's people had heard every word both men said, and they looked at him with disgust on their faces. There had to be some way to show them he wasn't who Hamish and Shamus claimed he was. That he wasn't here to take from them, to rule over them, to be the lazy ass, useless piece of shit the other Ian Mackay had been. The question was, though, how?

He scanned the horizon and breathed in a lung full of crisp, salty sea air as inlet waves crashed upon seal strewn rocks at the end of a protected cove and the occasional sea gull flew overhead, speckling a gray cloud-covered sky.

In his mind, Ian could almost hear the spokesman from WSYX channel six news out of Columbus, Ohio say, "It looks like a blustery one today folks. You might want to take an umbrella along, just in case those overcast skies decide to leak on you."

His father had loved to listen to that particular station. Weatherman Bill had always been the family's favorite meteorologist for as long as Ian could remember.

A sudden wave of homesickness caught him off guard, and he reeled from it. Granted, he'd been with both his mother and father only moments before he'd left to pick up the seed corn and hog feed. That had been only days ago, to his way of thinking. But a lot had happened between then and now. What still felt like no more than a matter of a few days had become almost four hundred years and an entirely different lifetime ago, or really yet to come since he was living in the past.

His head hurt with the complexity of the situation, and he rubbed his forehead in an attempt to clear the cobwebs his brain felt loaded down with. He couldn't afford to let Shamus, Hamish, Aila, and especially the villagers see he was out of his element and not completely in control of his faculties, or, god-forbid, afraid. A good soldier never showed fear, not even when he was shitting himself. And Ian had been a very good soldier. Right up to the point where he'd gotten a good part of his squad killed.

So this was his land, his castle, his village?

He concentrated on surveying his surroundings. A sprinkling of thatched roof buildings sat off in the distance to his right. The village was situated nicely in a wind protected cove complete with seals sunning themselves upon the rocks of the beach. There were two nice sized fishing boats moored close by.

So these people were fisherman it seemed.

That was better than being a stinking farmer, but probably not by much.

To his left stretched fields, grasslands, hills, and rocky cliffs for as far as the eye could see. Very rocky cliffs, and very uneven fields and grasslands. So poorly maintained, as a matter of fact, no plow would ever be able to quickly turn that dirt over. The green of early spring grass was at least popping up here and there, and it did add some much-needed color to the dab brown of the mud. It really was a beautiful place, even though the ground appeared to be more sand than rich soil.

Ian chuckled to himself. Leave it to a farmer's son to notice the piss-poor quality of the damn dirt.

He took a deep breath and blew it out.

So what if he was four hundred years in the past? So what if he was married to a complete stranger? So what if the castle this body's original owner had been promised wasn't quite what he envisioned? He could make this work. Really, he could.

And so what if the Mackay clan's enemies were right on his doorstep and breathing down his neck? He was a soldier. He knew how to deal with men of war. So what if the original Ian Mackay's laird hadn't liked him and hoped he'd fail? For this Ian Mackay didn't give a rusty fuck what Laird William thought about anything, and he didn't have any intentions of failing. He'd known the sting of failure up close and personal. He didn't like it and wasn't about to repeat it anytime soon.

He had a wife to care for, a promise to keep to Fate, and friends to bring back from the dead when this job was said and done. Failure wasn't an option.

Ian took another deep breath. He could and would survive here. They all would. Not only would they survive, but they'd thrive. There were abundant natural resources at hand and people to work the land and sea. He could do this. He could rebuild the castle, see these people fed properly, and even perhaps surprise them all with a few new things they'd never seen before.

For the first time since opening his eyes in the year 1643, Ian Mackay smiled, really smiled as he leaned down and picked up one rock and then another.

Over his shoulder, he called out to Aila, "Put a kettle on the fire, wife, and get a stew brewing with whatever food we have left. We've people to feed if they're willing to lend a hand at making our home at least habitable for the night."

****

Aila shook her head. How could these, gentle folk, not realize they were being taken in by a *sidhe*? It was as if he'd mesmerized them all with his smile. For without exception, each man, woman, and child listened intently to every word Ian Mackay said and then tripped over each other for the chance to do his bidding.

If Aila had doubted for even a moment her husband truly was more fae than flesh and blood, watching him interact with the villagers and them interact with him had certainly cured her of that misconception.

Aye, the man was magical. For the moment, Shamus and Hamish had remounted their horses and headed back to give their report to Laird William, the villagers had begun to act as if Ian had been their laird for years and years and years.

People who didn't know him from Adam, normally untrusting highlanders who'd never heard his name or saw his face before this day, took a knee, swore their loyalty, and sought his favor. Women brought food from their own meager stores to add to the stew, and men fetched their tools in order to work right beside him. Boys carted stones from the fields to repair walls, and young girls gathered rushes to make their new laird and lady a proper bed.

But then Aila had to admit, she was almost as taken in by her husband as the villagers. And when he'd proudly led her inside their new home and showed her the progress made in just one afternoon, she'd been more than a little tempted to jump in his arms and properly show him her gratitude.

But she hadn't. There'd been too many eyes upon them.

She was amazed, though. When they'd first arrived at Borve, she'd wanted to cry. Most of the roof was caved in and not a single wall was without at least one large hole. The pantry was long bare, the fireplace broken and blocked with debris, and what furniture there'd once been had long ago been reduced to a pile of sticks. Though there was certainly still a long way to go, at least for tonight, they would have a dry roof over their heads, sweet smelling rushes beneath their tired bones, and food in their bellies. What more could any new bride ask for?

Except for the fact that she herself felt completely useless. There really wasn't much she could do to help with the rebuilding. Her skills in that area were nonexistent. Fergus had always felt menial labor was below the sister of the laird, so though she could sew a pretty stitch, if it was demanded of her, she didn't have the first clue as to repairing a stone wall. The last thing she wanted to do was take from these people who obviously had so little to share and not give back in return.

Then a young lad no older than seven or eight walked past her carrying stones for the wall and she knew exactly what she could do to help. He was a scrawny little thing, but loud, tight-sounding coughs wracked his small frame with each step. His dark hair lay limp and plastered to his forehead from exertion. His face, though smudged with dirt, was much paler than any child's should be, and that was taking in consideration this was still early spring and he'd probably not seen much sunshine for quite some time. His nostrils flared with each breath he drew, and his lips were tinted an unnatural shade of blue.

Aila grabbed her bag of herbs—her most prized possession—with one hand, and the child with the other.

"Come with me," she ordered as she pulled him

toward the fire.

Once there, she motioned for him to sit while she sorted through her bag. Finally, she added what she'd been looking for into a small kettle, filled it with water, and placed it beside the simmering stew.

"I need ta get these stones ta the laird," the child wheezed. "He's waiting on them."

She shook her head. "He can wait. How long have ye been sounding like that?"

The little boy stared at her. "Long as I 'member, I guess. Worse when stuff starts coming up out of the ground and when the leaves come back on the trees. I don't mind it, though. Old Amos says it's me due, 'cause I'm bad luck. Me mam died birthing me, and me da not long after her."

Aila's heart constricted in her chest. "The same thing happened to me, but that does nae make either one of us bad luck. It just makes us unfortunate."

The little boy laughed, and it started another coughing spell. When he could finally speak again, he smiled. "I do nae mind being bad luck. Folks leave ye alone when ye are. But ye can't mean it when ye say ye are unfortunate. Ye are wife ta the laird. Ye are verra lucky indeed."

"What are ye called," Aila asked as she poured the steaming brew of horehound with a pinch of her precious eucalyptus into a cup and handed it to the child. Found only in the southernmost reaches of Scotland, the leaves of what the locals called white ash were coveted by healers far and wide for their effect with breathing ailments. It was the only thing she had ever asked of her brother when he'd make his yearly trip to Glasgow. It was the one thing he'd always brought home to her even though he never agreed with her being a healer.

"I'm Daniel." He sniffed the concoction, took a small sip, and then grimaced.

"Drink it," she admonished. "And breathe in the fumes while you're at it. They'll help with what ails ye. Just ye wait and see."

****

So much for the Mackay clan motto of *with a strong hand*. There wasn't a single hand of any kind doing work right now. Where had all his help gotten off to?

Ian glanced around what would probably be an impressively large room when the work was all said and done and twiddled his thumbs. He'd been waiting for more rock to shore up the ruined fireplace for the better half of an hour, and not so much as a pebble had been delivered.

Did highlanders have a set quitting time when it came to manual labor? The clansmen's union or something to that effect? Were they at home sitting around their fires enjoying their evening meal while he stood around like an idiot, waiting? After all, they wouldn't know to tell him about a particular quitting time, would they? On the contrary, they'd expect him already to be aware of the rules.

There were obviously many things he still needed to learn about this strange country and time he was now a resident of. For when it came to work and work ethic, the original Ian Mackay's memories were certainly no help at all. If it didn't involve fighting or drinking or whoring, there was little or no information to draw upon, let alone something as menial as what practices the common man followed on any given day of the week.

Ian sighed. One thing was certain. He wasn't going to get any answers standing around here all evening. So he did the only thing left for him to do. He dusted off his hands and headed back outside. The very first sight that met his glance stopped him dead in his tracks.

It was Aila, but not the scared, timid, quiet little Aila he'd known her to be so far. Or even the raging one, accusing him of being a fucking fairy.

Oh no. This Aila wasn't scared or timid or the least bit quiet or anything else negative right now. The woman standing no more than a few feet away was vibrant, animated, and so far beyond simply beautiful that the word didn't begin to describe.

Firelight danced around her and illuminated her profile, from the bright red, untamed curls atop her head to the intense moss-green of her eyes, to the wide, luscious smile upon her delicate elfin face. She was perfection. And as tiny windblown embers of that self-same fire danced about her arms and legs, she herself became the magical creature she accused him of being. Oh yes. If anyone was fae, it was Aila Mackay.

The people, his people, her people, they grouped about her, hanging onto every word she spoke and every gesture she made. He started toward her. He couldn't help himself. He was just as drawn as everyone else and even more than a little jealous. She was his, *his* wife, after all, not theirs. She shouldn't be smiling at other men the way she was, and she shouldn't be reaching out and touching them or bending down to listen to what they had to say.

She looked up and caught him watching her, and

the magic that was Aila ground to a sudden halt. The smile left her lips at the same exact second the excitement faded from her eyes and dread filled them. Her arms went limp, her bouncy red curls seemed to droop, and what felt like a thousand pairs of watchful eyes turned their accusatory gaze upon him.

"Am I interrupting something?" Ian asked.

Her chin came up a notch. "Nae. I was just seeing ta our folk as any good lady would do. They've had nae healer since theirs died." She pointed to a small child sitting close by. "Wee Daniel here had a verra bad cough and needed a draught."

Ian glanced toward the child.

Daniel? What the fuck?

Of course, there had to be a Daniel among the group. Wasn't there always?

His heartbeat tripled, his palms began to sweat, and the air caught in his chest as the image of his best friend drawing his last breath came to mind, and he reeled from it. What right did this dirty little kid have to the name when the only Daniel that would ever matter could answer to it no more?

Even worse, the kid looked way too much like the one from his nightmares of Afghanistan. Those same dark, terrified, pleading eyes, that same dirt-smudged face, the same too-skinny little arms and too-loose hanging clothes, but this time, thankfully without...

Ian turned away. He couldn't stand to look at the child. But the sound of distress in Aila's voice had him turning back around a second later.

"It's nae their fault," Aila cried. "Do nae blame these people for me actions. I was only trying ta help, ye ken?" She gestured toward a group sitting close by.

Maxine Mansfield

"All these men, who have worked hard for ye all day, mind ye, had cuts and bruises that needed tending before they festered."

She pointed toward a young mother cradling an infant. "And this is Elspeth. Her babe has a fever and is fussy from cutting teeth. Ye certainly can't begrudge her me help. Especially since her mother, Agnes, will be our cook as soon as we have a kitchen up and running again. Just as she was for the old laid before the Sutherlands killed him."

She stuck out her chin even farther than it already had been, but the slight quiver of it gave away her nervousness. "I'll nae sit idly by and watch suffering when I can do something about it, Ian Mackay. I'm telling ye right now, I won't, so do nae be asking it of me."

For a heartbeat, Ian was stumped. Who'd made Aila feel she needed permission to help people? But then he knew. It had been her brother and his overly controlling ways. Well, she wasn't a Gordon anymore. She was a Mackay, and she didn't have to answer to Fergus ever again or ask permission of anybody.

Instead of saying any of the things running through his mind, he simply held out his arm in order to show her the deep nasty cut he'd figured to patch up himself when he got the chance.

"I'm not questioning your motives, lass. Trust me. I'm thankful you're willing to help." He winked and gloried in the blush that spread up her neck and across her cheeks. "I was just hoping for a little of your attention myself. If it's not too much trouble, that is."

Chapter Seven

Familiar sounds floated through Ian's mind, and he fought not to open his eyes. Not again, not again. Please, God, not again. But just like a thousand times before his eyes did open to random people in strange clothing walking about, gesturing and speaking to each other in a language he couldn't quite comprehend. Somewhere a child cried, dogs barked, an engine hummed, and an explosion went off in the distance.

He cringed. Why tonight of all nights?

It wasn't as if he didn't know exactly where his dream had taken him this evening. He was back in the middle of the dry-ass, fucking Afghanistan desert, on patrol again. Danny was by his side, very much alive and smiling at him, trusting him, laughing with the other men, Kent, Andrew, and Ariel. They all behind the wheel of their Humvee. Danny was their driver, of course, just as he'd been back home on almost any given Saturday night, cruising Township Road 59 from North Woodbury through Johnsville, trying to pick up chicks.

The only real difference being, that now, instead of chasing tail, they were hunting insurgents on the other side of the fucking world.

He tried to swallow and couldn't.

Ian's mouth went dry, his tongue stuck to the roof of his mouth, and his teeth felt so gritty they reminded him of sandpaper. Not to mention the added layer of sand coating the inside of his nose, along with every other orifice he was in possession of. The combination made breathing, sitting, and especially concentrating not an easy task.

Not that he really wanted to breathe very deep anyway. Taking in a deep gulp of Afghanistan air this close to a village meant exposing himself further to the cultural ambiance of diesel fuel laced with the odor of raw human waste. Not to mention the added mixture of burning trash, oil smoke, dust from all that freaking sand, combined with a whiff of the spices used in today's cooking of whatever animals they'd happened to have slaughtered in the last few days.

Then, of course, there were the camel smells heaped on top of all that. The spiting, biting, piss-poor excuse for horses smelled like they'd been rolled thoroughly in fermented urine and baked until ripe in the hot desert sun for weeks.

Even slopping those nasty-ass hogs at home, day in and day out, hadn't been half as bad as one fucking lung full of Afghanistan.

Not that he should've had the window down in the first place. He should have known better. Everyone who was anyone knew it was much more prudent to roast to death in the enclosed cab of a Humvee than be blown to smithereens from a random IED.

But like every time before, tonight's dream was way too much like the real thing. Right down to the memory of the sting of biting sand fleas around his ankles, to the fear of scorpions lying in wait while he slept with his face buried in a dug-out sand hole at night, to the dog-sized rats running rampant everywhere one looked.

The hot sun bore down upon the bullet proof glass of the vehicle, blinding him with its glare, and that didn't help matters. Neither did the trickle of sweat running along his spine. His heart pounded hard in his chest, and the desperate need to open the door and jump from the Humvee had his legs aching with the desire to do just that. He knew what was about to happen. He'd lived and relived it at least a thousand times. He had no desire to do so again.

If only the vehicle would turn around just this once. They weren't even supposed to be this far into the village. At least not in this section of this village. It had taken only the one wrong turn to put them here. Right dab in the middle of a well-documented hot spot.

But they couldn't and wouldn't turn around.

Like every other time, the narrow dirt and gravel road of the alleyway they traveled prevented it. That and the fucking dogs, camels, and people meandering in the middle of the make-shift road.

God, what he wouldn't give for a blessed moment of fresh cold air upon his face before all hell broke loose. And for the chance to, just once, change what was about to happen.

Instead, there was a momentary stillness, like death itself, right before the hell he knew was coming began.

It was supposed to be just another routine patrol, easy-peasy. Three Humvee's, fifteen men, and about an hour's time. He wasn't even supposed to be with them today. The lieutenant had volunteered to lead this mission because Ian hadn't had more than six hours at a time off for days on end. At the very last moment, the lieutenant had been called away, and Ian, always ready to do his duty, had been more than glad to take his place.

He'd even been proud of himself for volunteering. After all, he was a marine, and rest was for the weak or the dead.

He'd trained for and was close to testing for his E7. Stepping up would look good on his record.

He was ready for whatever Afghanistan could throw at him.

Or at least he'd thought he was.

What a mistake that'd been. No matter how hard he prayed it wouldn't be, each time the nightmare played out, the ending was exactly the same.

Up ahead, he saw the intersection getting closer and closer. On both sides of the narrow, gravel street, people wandered to and fro, doing whatever people do. Dogs barked, open market vendors sold their wares, and music that wasn't country blared. In a matter of heartbeats, men who'd been counting on him, and worst of all, his best friend in the whole freaking world, would be reduced to a mass of mangled bloody body parts strewn all over the fucking desert.

He'd relived the memory so many times over the past three years that he knew every single second of every single thing that was about to happen. He also knew no matter how hard he tried, he couldn't and wouldn't change a thing. Not during this nightmare anyway. It wasn't within his power.

Just around the next corner, a kid once more darted out into the middle of the road. He was probably seven, maybe eight. His dark brown hair hung limp in his dirty, little face. His eyes were wide with fear. His ridiculously large white shirt lay wide open, a neat little row of C4 bricks all linked together with red and black wires circumventing his torso. The entire contraption was strapped snuggly to his small middle. The child held a detonator gripped tightly in his small right hand.

On cue, Danny turned toward him. "Damn, would you look at that, Ian? I can't just run the kid down like I know I should. Not with explosives strapped to him. You're gonna have to take him out."

And just like every other time, Ian did look. He couldn't not look, and he couldn't look away.

He looked so closely at the fear in the boy's eyes that he watched a single tear slip down the kid's dirty little face in slow motion a mere moment before Ian lifted his rugger and aimed.

Ariel, the turret-gunner, shouted "Incoming"

A split second later, the whole-wide-world exploded around them.

Ian was still watching the child when the blast threw him clear, and smoke and pain filled his lungs to the point he couldn't breathe. That was the last thing he remembered before waking up in the army hospital two weeks later.

Again, always and forever again, he'd failed, and Danny, Ariel, Kent, Andrew, and god only knew how many of his men in the other two Humvees were dead.

If only he'd pulled that trigger.

****

He awoke with a start. Smoke from the peat fire across the room burned his nostrils and made his eyes water while the sound of his clansmen's snores reverberating off the walls made him want to jump right out of his skin. Tomorrow, he'd work on the stairs and the master's chamber, so he and his wife could at least get a moment's peace and quiet.

As for tonight, luckily Aila slept on. But there'd be no more rest for him. He was always antsy after the dream. On top of it, he had questions running through his mind. Questions he desperately needed answers to, and there was only one person he could think of who might actually have them.

Dressing as quickly and silently as possible, he headed out the door. The moment he was free of the castle grounds, he broke into a full out sprint.

"Tobias," Ian whispered into the darkness when he finally reached a spot he thought would be safe. "Fate, you conniving, little bastard, show yourself. I know you can hear me."

Wind whipped around his bare legs and up his kilt. He shivered.

He hadn't wanted to leave the warmth of Aila's body tucked in close to his, run what felt like a mile, and certainly not climb over huge rocks and get sprayed by cold-ass sea water, but he had to make sure he was far enough from the castle and his much too observant little wife so he wouldn't be seen talking to a strange little man in a fucking white robe.

She already thought him brought back to life and possessed by the fairies. The last thing he needed was for her to see him talking to someone who looked like one.

But a chat with Tobias Moiré was exactly what Ian had in mind before he could even start formulating plans for any of their futures.

"Tobias," he hissed. "I'm not kidding. You said you'd be here when I needed you. Well, I need you now."

The air around him began to shimmer. "You just might want to change your tone when speaking to a celestial being, Ian Mackay. I am not now, nor have I ever been a bastard. I am a Moiré, a direct descendant of the original three Fates, and as such, most assuredly not to be mocked or ridiculed."

The shimmering light began forming into a solid. "If I was of a mind to, I could snap my fingers, whip up a tidal wave, and wash your entire castle away. You just might want to keep that in mind. And speaking of natural disasters, do you have any idea what you just interrupted? This had better be the most important needing in the history of all needings ever."

Ian blinked twice. Though he'd been the one to summon Tobias, the sight of his shaggy brown hair, wire-rimmed glasses, and white robe still surprised him. He shuffled his feet once as his hands sought pockets to jam them into before he remembered he was wearing a kilt instead of jeans and didn't have any.

He settled for stiffening his spine and looking Fate straight in the eye. "Nice to see you, too. If I remember correctly, you told me if I needed anything, just call, so I am."

Tobias rolled his eyes. "I'll have you know, I was in the middle of brewing up a blizzard, a big one. And since it's the beginning of spring, it won't be expected and will catch countless souls unprepared. Is what you *need* more urgent than that?"

Ian shook his head. "Don't you ever get tired of causing mischief?"

Fate harrumphed. "Do I tell you how to keep a squad safe? Oh wait, you already failed at that one, didn't you? Moving on."

Ian cringed. "You truly are a rat bastard."

Tobias smiled. "Tsk, tsk. Has no one ever told you fate is rarely kind?" He tapped his foot. "So what is it you need? I'm a very busy man, and I don't have time for *I need I need I need* pity parties."

The fingers of Ian's right hand itched to curl into a fist and punch Fate right in the nose. That wouldn't get him answers, however, so he resisted. "There are probably at least sixty people or more living on these lands. How am I supposed to keep them all safe and fed? I'm one man, and the Sutherlands breathing down our backs are basically endless. How long do I have to do this job before I earn the right to go back and have another try at what happened to that squad of mine? A week? A month? A year? Ten fucking years? A hundred?"

Ian clenched and unclenched his fists, the desire to hit something, anything, almost overwhelming.

"Oh, and by the way," he added. "You neglected to tell me Aila saw the original Ian Mackay dead. She thinks I'm possessed by the fairies." He gestured wildly. "Fairies of all fucking things. What am I supposed to do about that? It's not like I can tell her the truth."

Tobias chuckled. "Tell her whatever you wish to tell her. It's not as if she's going to believe you anyway." He chuckled again. "So she truly thinks you're a fairy, huh? Now that's what I call justice. You humans really are quite the whiny, needy things at times. You do know that, don't you?"

It was on the tip of Ian's tongue to tell Fate just where he could put his justice when the old man raised his hand. "I must admit I did know the girl saw the first

78

Ian dead. I didn't tell you because I was hoping she'd simply think it'd been a bad dream when she saw you alive and well the next morn."

"You see, in the original history," Fate continued, "her brother had her executed for the Mackay lad's death. It just so happens Hamish saw her fleeing Ian Mackay's room the night before. Both the Sutherland and the king demanded she be put to death or the entire Gordon clan would pay the price. Fergus had no choice but comply."

Tobias shrugged. "Not that it matters now, but I didn't believe he even truly minded at the time. Didn't shed a single tear, you see. Simply had her remains burnt after the deed was done and walked away. Though he himself was found dead just a few days later. Some suspected by his own hands. Couldn't handle the guilt, I suppose."

Ian shuddered, but he wasn't surprised, and he certainly hoped that Aila's brother had taken his own life after taking hers. The only person who probably deserved the title of rat-bastard more than Fate was Fergus Gordon.

"But since in this history, you didn't die and neither did she or Fergus," Tobias continued. "I suppose having Aila think you fae isn't the worst thing that could've happened. Time will take care of the problem. It always does. Just you wait and see."

The air around them began to shimmer once more. "And as for how you'll feed and protect those who are counting on you and for how long? My answer is this. For as long as it takes, of course. And you'll do whatever works. You were raised a farmer, so be a farmer and feed them. You were trained as a soldier, so be a soldier and protect them."

Ian couldn't believe it. Fate was doing it again. Just disappearing in the middle of a conversation. "But—but—but—"

Tobias flickered for a moment. "That's all the time I have for you right now. That blizzard won't wait forever, you know. Call if you need, but only if you really, truly, your-life-depends-upon-it needs. I can't be holding your hand all the time, you know."

And with that, Tobias Moiré, third generation event manipulator, better known as Fate, completely disappeared.

"Who ya talking ta, laird?"

Ian almost jumped out of his skin a heartbeat before whirling around and glaring at the owner of the voice. "What are you doing out here in the middle of the night, kid? Shouldn't you be at home asleep?"

The dirty-faced little urchin had the audacity to stick out his chin. "Ye talk verra strange. And I'm on the lookout for Sutherlands. Somebody's gotta, ye ken? So who was ye talking ta, laird."

Ian was almost tempted to tell the little boy who shared his best friend's name just who he'd been talking to and scare the shit out of him. It'd serve the creepy little kid right for being so nosy and sneaking up on him. But with his luck, he'd probably be bombarded with even more stupid questions. So he settled for, "If you must know, I was talking to myself. Now go back to bed. It's the middle of the night."

Daniel giggled, and it made him cough. "Old Amos says folks who talk ta themselves are titched in the head."

Ian gave him the glare he normally saved for

grown-ass soldiers he had no intentions of arguing with. When he gave an order, he meant for it to be followed. "I said go back to bed."

The child's lip quivered, but at the same time, his chin came up another notch. "I understand ye are the new laird and all, and I don't wish ta disobey ye, but a Sutherland killed the old laird while the whole village slept. I keep watch every night now. 'Tis a blood oath I took."

Ian wanted to point out to the kid that someone as small as he couldn't possibly be much good against a full-grown Sutherland if he did happen to come across one, but he didn't have the heart. So he settled for stating the obvious. "Isn't that the guardsmen's job?"

This time Daniel's eyes widened in surprise. "What guardsmen? Ye mean the old laird's men? 'Cause if'n ye do, they left after he was kilt. Said they weren't gonna stay and lose their lives for a bunch of smelly fishermen and their ale wives. But I don't mind. I'll keep watch, laird. Ye'll see. I'm nae afraid of no ole Sutherland."

Something about this Daniel reminded Ian of his best friend. He had the same bravery that went beyond his years, beyond reason, and after what Ian had contemplated doing in Afghanistan to that other little boy, he didn't have the heart to argue with this one. So, instead of trying to send the kid back to bed once more, he brought himself to full attention and saluted the child. "Then Semper Fi and carry on soldier. May your watch be uneventful. But starting tomorrow, I'll see to it you have some grown up help whether you think you need it or not."

Daniel giggled again. "Ye really do talk verra

strange, laird. What's a Semper Fi, and what's a soldier?"

Ian bent until he was eye level with the child. "Where I come from, Semper Fi is what one marine says to another. It means unending loyalty, and a soldier is someone who keeps watch while others sleep. Soldiers are the laird's right-hand men when he needs them to be. They're the ones the laird can depend on like no others. They have his six and can be trusted with the very hardest of tasks. You are now one of my soldiers. If you want the job, that is."

A wide smile broke across Daniel's face, and tears glistened in his eyes. He nodded rapidly. "Ye may verra well be titched in the head, and even though I do nae ken everything ye say, I know I can be a good soldier, laird. I swear I can."

Ian didn't dare stick around long enough to hear another word the young boy said. He couldn't. He wouldn't. He knew better.

He might kind of like the little kid's gumption. He might even see a bit of his old friend in him, but he'd never again be stupid enough to allow his emotions to get the better of him. Especially not with some snot-nosed little boy about the same age and size as the one he'd had in the cross-hairs of his M16 in Afghanistan and failed to put down in time.

No, he'd never allow himself to become that weak, that vulnerable again. He'd learned that particular lesson the hard way. Letting something as stupid as feelings for those smaller and weaker, those who were not his direct responsibility, interfere with the job at hand brought nothing but torment, heartbreak, pain, and grief.

Better to remain the coward he, and only he, knew himself to be.

Better to stay aloof.

Better to not let them in.

Chapter Eight

June 1643
Borve Castle

If the man truly wasn't a *sidhe* as he claimed, she'd sure like to know exactly what he was. One thing was for certain. Ian Mackay could not be merely mortal. No man could go as long as he had with so little rest and still be just another living, breathing soul upon God's green earth.

Aila watched Ian work and shook her head. He'd been at it almost nonstop from dawn till dusk for the better part of a sennight. The only time she'd seen her husband without a tool or sword in his hands had been when he'd sat down to quickly eat a meal and the few moments at bedtime when he'd held her in his arms as she fell asleep, frustrated.

But always, without fail, sometime in the middle of the night, he'd jump up and be gone.

When she went looking for her errant husband, in the daytime anyway, she'd without fail find him trying to make fighting highlanders out of fishermen. Or at times, repairing yet another hole in one of the walls or roofs or attempting to build something, anything else. But that was when he wasn't giving orders to the lads clearing fields of rocks as to where to stack them. Or talking with the blacksmith, the sheepherder, the stable master, or any one of at least ten other chores he seemed to think were his and his alone. And that was when he wasn't inspecting fields, overseeing disputes between villagers, listening to complaints, or out hunting one of the scarce red-tail deer the highlands were famous for, in the hopes of filling all their bellies with something other than dried fish or seal.

It wasn't as if she got the chance to talk with him privately if and when she did find him. For even if he wasn't in the middle of a conversation with someone else, where she saw Ian Mackay, she inevitably saw wee Daniel. The wean stuck so close to his laird she'd be hard-pressed to slide a single piece of straw between the two of them.

The thought brought a much needed smile to Aila's face.

Though Ian grumbled incessantly about his little shadow, she'd seen the fleeting expressions of tenderness directed toward Daniel when the boy wasn't looking, when no one else was looking. She'd noticed the extra portion of food he sneaked on the lad's trencher each evening, taken from his own. And she'd been witness to more than a few of their conversations and couldn't help but marvel at Ian's patience in explaining even the simplest of details.

And the lad?

Daniel basked in every moment of attention Ian gave him. His cheeks were now a healthy pink, and so were his lips. Aila had hardly heard him cough or wheeze for days, and when she did, it certainly wasn't anything like when they'd first arrived. As a matter of fact, she hadn't had to give him the eucalyptus concoction again. Perhaps she was simply getting used to the sight of him, but he even seemed bigger. As if the few supplemented meals already were putting much needed weight on his wee frame.

She smiled again, and of their own volition her hands came to rest upon her abdomen. Ian Mackay would make a wonderful father if given the chance. And oh, how she longed to be a mother. Even though her mum died birthing her, it was still a dream to have and hold a babe of her own. She'd helped birth dozens of wee ones and placed them in their mother's arms. But at her advanced age of twenty-two, she'd all but given up on the idea of ever having one of her own.

Her smile faded. Even if Fergus hadn't threatened to kill any bairn she had with Ian, *sidhe*s weren't capable of fathering children. Everybody knew that. But then he swore he wasn't a *sidhe*. Over and over, Ian had told her she was mistaken in what she thought she'd seen.

Could he be right? He'd certainly looked dead that night she found him. He'd certainly felt dead when she poked him. And though it was probably the vomit, he'd most certainly smelled dead, too.

Not that it really mattered if he was a *sidhe* or no. One thing she knew without a doubt was, if she didn't lie with her husband, she would not have weans, and Ian Mackay hadn't so much as touched her hand let alone anything else, at least not in that particular way, since they'd first lain together.

Not that she could blame him. He no doubt found her as scrawny and unattractive as the men of her clan had. After all, how many times had Fergus taunted her and told her she looked more like a half-grown lad than she did a woman? How many times had he laughed and said a real man needed a woman with meat on her bones? A woman of substance. A woman built to give a man big-sturdy sons. A woman like Rhona.

For a time she'd tried eating everything she could get her hands on, but her hips still didn't widen even a tiny bit, her breasts didn't plump up, and her belly remained as flat and unwelcoming as the stones on the bottom of the river bed. Eventually, she'd simply given up trying. She'd had no choice but to accept the fact she was who she was and couldn't change it.

She wasn't exactly ugly either. More than one braw highlander had told her she was bonny in her own way. Even though her hair was an unruly mass of red curls and her curves basically non-existent, it wasn't as if she hadn't ever been kissed before the day Ian Mackay wed her either. For she had, twice as a matter of fact. Once by the Sutherland's great nephew, and then again by Lachlan Gordon, who'd been a visiting cousin.

In the end, neither man had offered for her. Part of the reason might have been that they didn't want to give Fergus what he'd been asking, but Aila had no doubt they'd also looked at her and decided she wasn't quality breeding stock.

She sighed. Could she even blame Ian for not wanting to waste his time bedding her?

But she so very much wanted to bed him.

The memory of his warm hands and lips and tongue upon her body, kissing her, licking her, sucking the place between her thighs thrumming with need. Just the thought of the size of him and the fact that even though she'd been sure he wouldn't fit, he had. Not just fit but he'd slid that magnificent cock of his in and out and in and out, over and over, until she shattered into a million pieces right in his arms.

She wanted to do that again. She wanted to do that again very, very much, over and over and over again. But how, when the man refused to stop working long enough to even see the deed done before falling into a restless sleep then slipping out of their bed in the middle of the night and going only God knew where?

****

As she walked toward him, all Ian could think was, if Aila swished those sweet hips of hers for even one more step, his balls were going to turn from their already state of aching blue to near bursting indigo black, and there wasn't a damn thing he could do to stop it.

God, he wanted her, and no matter how hard or how long he worked each day, the need to touch her, taste her, take her, possess her, delve into her warm, wet depths and explode deep within her was driving him completely insane.

But after the disaster of his wedding day and what he'd had no choice but to trick her into, he felt so guilty that he made a promise to himself. He'd not make love with her again until he was without a doubt sure it was her idea and what she wanted. It was the only way he'd been able to live with the fact that he felt not even a shred of real regret for seducing a complete innocent, because it had been the single most enjoyable experience of his entire life.

Who could've blamed him? His wife was stunningly beautiful, after all. Pixie-like and delicate, from her cute little ears to her pouty little mouth, to her pert, perfect little breasts, to her tiny little feet with their ten tantalizing toes, she was everything any man in his right mind could've ever hoped or dreamed for.

He'd never seen the likes of her anywhere or in any other time. If this had been the twenty-first century, he had no doubt that she was the kind of woman he would've been standing and staring up at as she graced a billboard high above his head.

It wasn't only her outer features that attracted him either. Even though the sight of her brilliant red hair hanging loose and swinging about her sweet little ass in a mass of curls had his fingers itching at the thought of fisting a soft handful and holding on for dear life while plunging into her furiously.

His cock suddenly spasmed beneath his kilt, and he quickly covered the evidence of his weakness for her with his hand.

God, yes, his wife was pretty, but she was smart, too, and kind and talented and wise well beyond her years. Even if she was convinced he was some sort of fucking fairy.

Every day she surprised him more and more. She tended these people, these Mackays, who more often than not glanced her way with fear and mistrust in their eyes, and she did it just as if they'd been her family all her life instead of her clan's sworn enemy.

From the moment she rose in the morning until she fell asleep at night, she was always busy doing something. She comforted the sick and rocked colicky babies. She bandaged wounds and wiped runny noses. She made poultices and concoctions even *he* was afraid to ask the ingredients of. All of this before the sun was even high in the sky.

Then, when she was satisfied those in need were taken care of, she worked right beside the other women clearing fields, weaving wool, cooking food, mending sails for the fishing boats, and a hundred other small tasks he'd watched her do every day. She did it all without so much as a single word of complaint.

"That would probably be the southern-most field, laird. It's the farthest upwind, if'n ya ken what I mean."

Ian quickly glanced back toward the man he'd forgotten he was conversing with only moments before Aila came into his view. Brody Mackay was a wiry, gruff old highlander of at least sixty years, if he was a day, but he was also the lead fisherman for the clan and a man with much useful knowledge to impart.

"And how far is that field from the loch," Ian asked.

The old fisherman chuckled. "Never measured it, but since the loch's on the south side of the village too, I suppose it's closer than it would be ta the fields ta the north."

Ian nodded. He'd thought of a plan to get at least one field ready for spring planting, and he'd just needed to know which field to choose. And since it looked like the most southern field was where last season's fish guts had been dumped, it'd be perfect. With all that natural fertilizer already in place, he'd only have to plow and seed it.

Excitement filled him. Finally, something was falling easily into place.

All week long, even what should've been simple easy chores had for one reason or another taken twice as long as they should've. With the castle, it had been the lack of quality mud to cement the rocks together. The land close by had been so sandy it was hard to get it to stick together no matter how much straw he added. So richer, thicker dirt had been brought in from farther inland, one tediously slow wagon full at a time.

The repairs to the boat's sails, after the long, harsh winter, had certainly been a chore. There hadn't been enough quality thread left to mend them properly. He'd solved that problem with an early spring shearing of the lambs, but again that in itself had taken time. Let alone the hull damage that had to be painstakingly repaired. Not on just their boat, either, but also on the one Sutherland vessel ported close by.

Not that it had been the Mackays responsibility to repair the Sutherland vessel in the first place, and Ian certainly hadn't blamed his men for grumbling about working on their enemies' fishing boat, especially when their own needed attention. But helping out their closest neighbors, even when those neighbors hadn't asked, was part of a bigger plan he'd been formulating for a while.

He could almost hear his mother's voice ringing in his ears. "You can catch more flies with honey than you can with vinegar, son. Always remember that." He had remembered. Right along with all those Sunday sermons of love thy neighbor as you love yourself and treat others as you'd have them treat you.

The Sutherland clan who owned that particular fishing vessel weren't the same sector of the clan who killed the old laird, but they were one of the Mackays' closest neighbors. From what the villagers said, their relationship had never been what anyone could consider friendly, but they also hadn't been adversaries. That was enough for now.

"Aye, that field is close enough ta the loch, I suppose," Brody laughed. "But ta my knowledge it's nae ever been cleared. It's just always been a convenient dumping ground for fish guts and such. So be warned, Old Amos might have a word or two ta say about ye planting anything in his fields, and trust me, he considers all the fields around Borve Castle as his. He's been the head farmer since he was a lad. Oh, and that particular field may have a rock or two ta be picked up and moved off ta the side, ye ken."

Ian sighed. Of course there'd be Old Amos to deal with right along with rocks. After all, was there a patch of ground anywhere in the entire country that wasn't plagued with both of those fucking things? So much for something, anything, finally going right.

****

Aila scrunched her eyes tightly closed and waited. Ian moved about their chamber, and any minute he'd climb into bed. Of course, he'd think she was already asleep when he did it. All the better to catch the man unawares.

This morning had been the last straw. After she overheard the women in the kitchen gossiping about how their laird fell asleep every night without ever tupping his skinny, little Gordon wife, she'd come up with a plan of her own. She might have been born and raised a hated Gordon, but she was a Mackay like the rest of them now, and this Mackay was going to show them their lady meant to be wife to their laird in more than just name.

She'd smiled right at them when she ordered cook to make an extra hearty fish stew with a generous helping of oysters for supper. She'd even done it with a wink, knowing full well they knew any Scot worth his mettle, no matter how tired, would be in the mood for a good romp after a belly full of those delicacies and wouldn't think twice about it.

She'd also ordered the very best *uisge beatha* Castle Borve had to offer be served with their meal this evening, because everybody knew a man well on his way to being in his cups didn't mind a frisky little game of tickle and tup when his warm, willing wife was within reach. That was one of the many things she'd learned from watching the goings on in her brother's keep.

And at her insistence, fresh rushes had been scattered upon the floor of their newly reconstructed, private chamber. She'd even sprinkled wildflowers among them to add to the ambiance. Though small, it was nice to have a room with a door they could use to shut out the rest of the world, if only for a short time.

After growing up in her brother's castle and always having her own chamber, trying to sleep in the great hall surrounded by grunting, farting men, giggling, moaning females, and other obvious sounds of couples mating and such had been almost impossible to get used to. Especially since her husband had shown no indication what-so-ever he'd like to do the same thing with her. On the contrary, every night he'd simply snored in her ear.

Come hell or high water, that was not happening tonight.

They had their private chamber, and though sparsely furnished with not much more than a rough frame with a straw mattress tossed on it, a single chair, and the small chest she'd brought with her, Aila was determined Ian would not get the chance to fall asleep tonight before she got the attention she so desperately needed.

She'd lit and then blew out at least a half dozen candles around the room, not sure which would be better. For him to glimpse her wide awake and willing or for him to discover that for himself in pitch darkness.

In the end, she'd simply stoked the fire in the fireplace, hoping the subtle light of the flames would accentuate her readiness without reminding her husband of how lacking in attributes she really was.

She'd even gone so far as to risk a lung fever by bathing in the still chilly waters of the loch earlier in the day, and she'd done it just because she'd noticed Ian occasionally wrinkling his nose when certain villagers walked by, especially the fishermen. She hadn't wanted him to find her offensive.

So, there she lay, waiting and holding her breath, as naked beneath the furs covering their bed as the day she'd been born. Not only naked, but needy.

How could Ian Mackay have shown her the pleasures found in the marriage bed and then act as if they were nae husband and wife at all since arriving at Castle Borve? Was he ashamed of her? Did he even care she was a laughing stock among his people?

Well, if that was what her husband thought was acceptable behavior, then he was in for a rude awakening. *Sidhe* or not, trying to avoid her or not, ashamed or not, exhausted from working all day or not, or even just plain not in the mood, she wasn't having it anymore. And she wasn't taking no for an answer tonight either. Her husband was going to tup her before the sun rose upon Scotland again, and that's all there was to it.

Aila snuggled farther beneath the furs and smiled as Ian silently climbed into the bed beside her.

Chapter Nine

God in heaven above, Aila was stark-assed naked, soft, sweet smelling, and rubbing her sleepy little body up against him as if she were an innocent little kitten searching for warmth and he a trustworthy source of heat.

She couldn't be more wrong.

Ian took a deep breath and counted to ten, and then to twenty. Perhaps he should find somewhere else to rest his weary bones. Or perhaps he should just sneak back downstairs and drink another tankard or two of that strong-ass, bitter Scottish whisky they'd had with supper. That way he could simply pass out and still keep his promise not to touch her until she was truly ready.

But then she leaned into him, sighed, and slid a sexy little leg up the outside of his thigh, before wrapping it securely around his hip. She giggled as her sweet little toes tickled the crack of his ass, and Ian shuddered as a sudden wave of desire rocked him to the core.

His cock hardened, his balls tightened, and he gulped.

"Does this give ye ideas, husband?" She giggled again.

Oh, he had ideas, all right. But all he could think was she must've had way too much to drink and it would be beyond wrong to take what was obviously being offered. Wouldn't it?

Reluctantly, he unwrapped himself from her arms and swallowed hard. "An honorable man doesn't take advantage of a woman when she's not quite herself. Especially if that woman happens to be his lady wife."

She had the audacity to giggle once more as she scooted right up against him again and ran her hand down his body and grasped his throbbing cock. "Nae even if yer lady wife wants ye to take advantage?"

He couldn't breathe, and he couldn't think. The feel of her small soft hand wrapped firmly around his hard shaft had his brain drawing blanks as to what to say next. The fact she was sliding that same hand slowly up and down had him on the verge of forgetting he'd ever made a promise to himself in the first place.

It took all the willpower he could muster to forcibly unwrap her hand and hold her at arm's length. "No, Aila, not like this."

She scrunched up her face into a pout. "Do *sidhe*'s nae enjoy tupping then, Ian?"

Irritation filled him. "How many times do I have to tell you? I'm not a fucking fairy. And trust me, I enjoy…tupping just as much as the next guy, thank you very much."

All humor left her face, even the sparkle that had been in her eyes moments before disappeared, and her voice became not much more than a whisper. "Well, if'n ye are nae a *sidhe* as ye claim, then why do ye nae want ta tup yer wife? I ken I'm nae as bonny as some, but am I really that frightful?"

Ian couldn't believe his ears. There was no way this beautiful, sexy woman could ever think herself not attractive. But she did. He could see it there in her eyes, a sadness, an insecurity, a to-the-core-hurt even.

He pulled her in close until her cheek rested upon his chest. "God no, you aren't in the least frightful. As a matter of fact, you are the opposite of frightful, Aila. You're the most gorgeous woman I've ever known. I just don't want to rush this. I feel like a creep for practically forcing myself on you on our wedding day."

She lifted her chin until she was looking straight up at him. "Ye are a strange man, Ian Mackay. But ye do nae need ta say false words ta me. I know I'm nae a beauty. Even if I hadn't been able ta see that for meself, me brither told me many times how lacking in womanly qualities I am. And ye did nae force yerself on me on our wedding day. Ye did yer duty ta king and country, and so did I. But bonny or frightful, I'm still a woman whose husband does nae touch her. And others are starting ta notice, too. I hear the whispers, and I see the looks of pity, Ian. Yer people think ye do nae tup yer wife 'cause ye can nae stand ta lay with a Gordon. And I'm feared they're right."

Ian rested his forehead on hers and smiled for the first time in what felt like forever. "Well then, wife, let me show you just how wrong you and they are."

****

The stroke of his fingertips across the small of her back was like a perfect mixture of fire and ice. Shivers of excitement skittered along Aila's spine while an all-encompassing heat wiggled its way to the center of her core, warming her from the inside out, teasing her with the promise of what was to come.

She sighed as his lips melded with hers. His tongue quickly darted out, intertwining with hers, playing a game of give and take, capture and release, paring, advancing, and retreating before attacking once again. He tasted of stout Scottish whisky, rich and warm and manly, with just a hint of northern barley left behind. He tasted of home, of safety, comfort, and belonging.

It was distracting, that tongue of his, and not simply distracting but quite deceiving. It had her believing for the first time in her life that perhaps she could be woman enough to merit a man's attention. Not just any man, but this man in particular.

If he still was a flesh and blood man, that was.

For a moment, she wondered if it was wrong to enjoy the touch of a *sidhe* so much and was his touch and his kiss so very intoxicating because he was a magical creature instead of a human being. But magical or not, the fact remained, he was her husband, and she craved his touch, hungered for it, had dreamed of it.

Aila admitted to herself she didn't care. She'd worry about her insecurities as to whether her husband was fae tomorrow. All that mattered right now was that this Ian Mackay, her husband, her laird, was making her feel verra bonny indeed…and cherished…and desired, just as a wife should be.

She smiled as she kissed him back enthusiastically, relaxing once more into his embrace, snuggling even closer, eager to enjoy every single moment of what was about to happen.

Then he did the strangest thing. He lifted her into his arms and carried her to the small chair close to the fire. He sat and positioned her facing him with her legs tucked in close on both sides of his hips, his rock-hard cock pulsating between them.

"If you truly wish this, my wife, then you take me.

Ride me at your pace and at your pleasure. I am yours to do with as you wish."

Her mind went blank. Take him, ride him? Did wives even do such things? And if so, how?

She gulped. "I do nae ken what ye mean, Ian."

The fingertips of his right hand playfully toyed with the crack of her ass, and she sucked in a breath as flames of desire coursed through her belly."

He nibbled her neck and chuckled as he slid his hands under her ass and gently lifted. "I mean, slide yourself down upon me, Aila. Take what you want. I am yours to do with as you will, always and forever."

Ian grasped one of her hands and brought it to his hot, hard flesh. "See how much I want you? Just the sight of you drives me crazy."

Slowly, she positioned her opening at the head of his cock and did as Ian instructed. She moaned as the first inch of his wonderful warmth entered her, and with a greed she wasn't even aware she possessed, she quickly slid down the length of him, marveling in the power of her position, humbled by the trust.

He'd given her a great gift, and he didn't even know it. No one had ever trusted her with pleasure.

They'd trusted her to ease their pain while sick or dying, and many had trusted her to heal their hurts and injuries, but no one had ever thought her capable of giving pleasure. She'd never been considered womanly enough.

Well, she was now.

With a smile, she rode him, experimenting with her pace and gauging her success by the sounds her handsome husband let slip from his oh-so-sexy lips. He groaned when she teased him with a slow and steady gait. All the way up until only the very tip of his luscious cock remained imbedded within her, and he moaned and gasped as she sped up to furiously pound herself upon his quivering flesh, over and over and over.

He was magnificent, and through the gleam of his eyes and the catch of his breath she saw he felt the same toward her.

It was intoxicating, this power. It was primal and intimate and oh so precious. Instinctively, she could tell he was close to his release. His entire body seemed to hum with an energy. His muscles rippled beneath her touch, his breath came in quick uneven spurts, and his marvelous cock grew even harder, broader, its veins pulsating within her with every beat of his heart.

Then his hands and lips were on her everywhere at the same time it seemed, touching, caressing, stroking, fondling every single inch until she forgot to think, forgot to breathe, and even forgot that she was supposed to be in charge.

Leaning forward, he captured a nipple in his mouth and sucked. Bursts of spectacular tiny tingles shot straight through her belly and down her spine before wrapping themselves around her clit and causing it to throb with intense spurts of delight.

And then he did the strangest thing.

He hooked an arm about her hips and slowly inserted a finger straight up her ass, matching the in and out motion his wonderful cock already accomplished.

She'd never considered such a thing. It was naughty. Lusciously, delectably naughty, and doubled the intensity of what his cock was already doing.

Aila lost her mind as pure emotion took over, and

spasms of intense pleasure rocked her to the core a mere moment before the warm wonderfulness of Ian's release deep within her own body told her he too had found his release.

He held her close as their breathing slowed and their bodies once more righted themselves. A smile, like a cat licking cream graced her lips and she knew it but didn't care. She'd satisfied her husband, and he'd more than satisfied her. *Sidhe* or no, they truly were husband and wife now.

She snuggled into his embrace as he once more lifted her into his arms and carried her to their bed. He laid her down gently, wrapped his arm about her waist, and kissed her forehead before sleepily whispering, "Night, love."

Another surge of excitement skittered through her. Was she truly his love?

Aila grinned into the darkness. She hoped she was. *Sidhe* or no, she was developing strong feelings for Ian Mackay. Perhaps the things Rhona had told her about marriage had been true, after all. Her sister-in-law had said a man and woman become one flesh when they become husband and wife, but Aila'd never really understood what that meant.

Well, she was beginning to understand now.

She stared at her sleeping husband and stroked his cheek. They really were developing a bond, or at least she hoped they were. If she had any say-so in the matter, tonight was only the beginning of a love that fairies and fae, or death itself, would never be able to end.

****

God, she was beautiful.

Through the flickering light given off from the fireplace flames Ian watched Aila sleep. Even though his fingers itched to touch her, stroke her, wake her, and make love with her once more, he didn't. It was still a good hour before sunrise, and just because he'd been awakened by one of his nightmares didn't mean he had the right to intrude on his wife's well-deserved rest.

That didn't mean he didn't want to.

He smiled. It had been his very first thought after rising from their bed, relieving himself, stoking the fire, and climbing back between their furs. It would be so easy to do. She'd been so damn receptive to his touch. All he'd need do was nuzzle her neck, tweak a nipple, or slide down and kiss her cute little belly button before surprising her with a much more intimate kiss.

His mouth watered, and his cock hardened. Still, he didn't touch her.

Ian knew exactly what Aila's days were like. She rose just as early as he and worked just as long and hard. There'd be time to make love with his beautiful wife when she woke come sunrise and before they both had to face their duties. That was all there was to it. He smiled into the darkness once more. Perhaps they'd even make a habit of it, their way of starting each new day.

For now, there were things he needed to decide, things he needed to work out. The ships were mended, which meant the fisherman could set out as soon as the seas permitted. The food stores were becoming dangerously low. Would there be enough to send along to feed the men on the ships without starving those left behind? The fields...how long would it take to clear even the one decent field for planting, let alone two or three? Especially if it meant arguing with Old Amos over every decision he made. Could quality grain even be grown in mostly sand? The sheep needed to be moved to fields with more grass, and stock needed to be taken of ewes and breeders versus wool bearing, and those who were no longer good for anything but the stewpot.

His head hurt, but it was better than thinking about his recurring nightmare of Afghanistan or the fact it would be wrong to wake his sleeping wife just because he really wanted to fuck.

He had a few coins to spend from the reward Laird William had given him for marrying Aila. How was he to get through Sutherland land, safely to Inverness and back, in order to spend them on much needed seed, livestock, and so many other things these people were sorely lacking?

It would be quicker and safer to simply go down the coast by ship, but they only had the one that truly belonged to them, and fish and the other bounties of the sea were too important to their existence to waste time on a supply trip. So, by horse and wagon it would have to be.

But how? They were surrounded to the north and east by the sea and to the west and south by Sutherlands.

God, what he wouldn't give for his old pickup truck right about now.

The thought brought a smile to his face, but a moment later, it faded as he remembered exactly what had happened to that truck and why he was in this predicament in the first place.

Ian could almost envision old Laird William,

sitting at his great table cackling with glee. Knowing full well he'd sent his useless nephew to his death and happy about it. This Ian Mackay wasn't the same Ian Mackay the old laird was angry at, though. Not that that mattered right now. He, Aila, and the people in their care would still suffer for the mistakes the first Ian had made.

There had to be a way, though. Fate wouldn't have put him in an impossible situation, would he? There had to be some way to make this work, to stave off their enemies, to see that these people not only survived but thrived, and somehow earn his way back to the day his squad had been killed.

There had to be a way. It was simply a matter of finding out how. And if anyone had the answers, it would be Tobias Moiré, third generation event manipulator, better known as Fate. This time, Ian had no intention of letting the little weasel slip away before penning him down to more complete answers than "Be a farmer and feed your people. Be a soldier and protect them."

He slipped out of his bed carefully so as not to wake Aila and dressed quickly before heading out the door. Sunrise was still at least a good hour away, and Fate wasn't going to get the chance to put him off this time.

Ian was almost to the castle door when it suddenly flew open and in ran a gasping and panting Daniel.

"Sutherlands, my laird," he wheezed. "There be at least a hundred filthy Sutherlands crossing our borders this verra moment, and they're heading this way."

The boy bent almost double, trying frantically to draw his next breath, and Ian rubbed his small back as he urged him to calm.

Fuck, this was the last thing Ian needed right now. But he'd also known that sooner or later the Sutherland problem would have to be dealt with. He'd just hoped to have more time to train his men, because most of these villagers were fishermen and farmers, not soldiers. After what had happened in Afghanistan, could he even ask another group of men to fight and die for him?

It seemed his conversation with Tobias would have to wait. He had a wife, a castle, a village, and a whole lot of people to protect, and he had no idea as to how to go about that. What he did know, however, was he had to somehow warn his fellow Mackays.

Ian waited another moment for Daniel to catch his breath. He felt guilty for sending the child back out into the night, but he patted him on the back and said, "Find old Brody, and the others. Tell them what's coming. Seek out every able-bodied man we have. Tell them to gather what weapons they have, be it only a club or a stick. But tell them not to attack unless I give the order. We will see what these Sutherlands want first. I'm counting on you, son."

Daniel nodded. "I'll do as ye wish, laird, but there is nae good Sutherland. What they want, what they always want, is Mackay blood."

Ian sighed. "Perhaps you're right, my young, brave soldier, but I'll still hear them out first. It's what a commanding officer does."

The boy shook his head. "Ye do speak verra strangely, my laird. Ye truly do."

****

There weren't a hundred Sutherlands, and of that,

Ian was very glad, but there were at least twenty. All of them right outside the gates leading to castle Borve and all mounted upon the ugly, short, shaggy horses the highlanders seemed to favor. To make the situation more interesting, they were, to a man, armed with bows, daggers, and claymores, especially their obvious leader while Ian and his men were equipped with the occasional sword, pick-ax, hatchet, and club.

Laird Stephen Sutherland as he'd grunted an introduction, was a giant of a man. Not someone Ian would've ever described as classically Scottish, their neighbor more resembled a prehistoric Neanderthal than anything else. But there was something about the man Ian trusted immediately. Something about the way the Sutherland laird looked him straight in the eye without wavering and without guile.

There was something else about those eyes, too. Something the soldier in Ian recognized. Sutherland was a man of war. A fact, Ian had the feeling, he'd not have to put to test today. Because whatever the reason for this unexpected visit and even though the Sutherlands were armed to the teeth, Ian would bet his left nut-sack this outing had nothing at all to do with attacking anyone. On the contrary, this was a man with a heavy heart and a big problem.

"I'll be speaking ta ye alone, if'n ye don't mind, Laird Mackay," Stephen Sutherland bellowed. "What I have ta say is private and nae fodder for wagging tongues."

Ian nodded and gestured toward the castle. He had no idea what was bothering the other man, but the least he could do was offer an ear to listen. "Then come and let's talk over food and drink. The sun's coming up, and it's time to break our fast."

The Sutherland dismounted and so did his men. When they started to follow, he raised his hand and shook his head. "Nae, stay here." They grumbled, but they did as their laird bid.

They hadn't even sat when Stephen came right to the point. "I have need of yer wife."

Ian just stared at him. What the fuck? He wasn't sure what he'd expected to hear, but it sure as hell hadn't been that.

The other man cleared his throat. "What I mean ta say is I have need of her skills. I did hear right, did I nae? She's the sister of Fergus Gordon, aye? The one rumored ta be a passably good healer?"

The fog in Ian's brain cleared slightly. "Yes. Yes, she is."

Stephen sighed with what looked to be obvious relief. "I need ta take her back ta my keep with me. My wife is close ta her time and swears something is wrong with the bairn and has need of her, even though she be a Mackay and our enemy." He had the decency to turn a nice shade of pink as the realization hit him he'd just insulted the man he was here to ask a favor of.

Ian simply chuckled. It was a good thing his lovely wife had put such a big smile on his face the night before. The last thing he wanted to do with anyone today was fight, not even with a Sutherland.

"We must leave right away, ye ken? If'n ye be willing, that is," Stephen continued. "We rode most of the night just ta get here, and it'll take the better part of the day ta get back. Enemies or nae, even a Mackay would nae put a babe at risk if'n he could help it. And I'll see her back safe and sound as soon as I can." He shuffled his feet and glanced back toward the door. "But we really do need ta get going."

It was on the tip of Ian's tongue to tell the Sutherland laird he'd be glad to ask his wife if she'd be willing when Aila walked into the room with her basket of herbs already on her arm. "Of course, I'll help." She then looked nervously toward Ian. "Won't I? May I?"

He wanted to wipe the uncertainty from her eyes. How could she think he'd prevent her from doing what she was meant to do? She had a gift when it came to helping people. He'd seen it numerous times since they'd arrived here, and he'd tried to let her know he believed in her, but it seemed in that aspect anyway, he'd failed, for his lovely little wife was still looking at him as if she needed his permission.

Ian cleared his throat, knowing the next words he said would be pivotal in their relationship for whatever time they'd have together. "You're a healer, Aila. You never have to ask for mine or anyone else's blessing to do what you're meant to do." He turned toward Stephen. "God's speed to you, but I'm afraid I can't go along with you this day. Don't worry about bringing my good wife back. I'll come for her myself. I simply can't leave before certain things are seen to. But trust that I'll follow as soon as I possibly can."

He hesitated for just a moment, then looked the other man straight in the eye. "I do have a favor to ask of you in return, though."

The Sutherland laird nodded. "If'n it's within my power, anything is yours."

Ian took a deep breath. "Safe passage for me and mine through Sutherland lands to Inverness and back. We've need of supplies."

Stephen nodded again. "Consider it done, and I'll ask the same of ye in kind. Safe passage here and back again so we can repair whatever damage the winter has done to my kinsman's ship, so our fishermen might set sail when the seas are finally calm enough once more and the fishing is good."

Ian smiled. "You're welcome to come and go as you please as long as your men cause no harm to my people, but as far as your ship, it's already been repaired and is ready to sail."

Stephen Sutherland narrowed his eyes. "Were ye meaning ta claim a Sutherland ship for yer own then? 'Cause if'n ye were, and though ye've agreed for yer wife ta aide mine, we'll have a wee problem, Mackay. My kinsmen need that ship, and the old Laird Mackay and I had a standing agreement. Will ye be breaking that trust, then? Are ye a thieving Mackay like so many of yer kinsmen?"

For a moment, Ian thought he should really be insulted, but he looked Sutherland in the eye again and could find nothing dishonorable about the man. It was simply another soldier, another laird, another desperate man, drawing a line in the sand at the feet of another.

"I neither want nor need your flea ridden excuse of a boat, Sutherland. We have a fine ship of our own. I simply noticed yours was in need of repair, and since we were already working on our own, we fixed that one, too. Like it or not, we're neighbors, even if our clans say we're supposed to be enemies. I know we both have many mouths to feed. If we help each other when we can, then maybe we'll both be able to do what needs to be done for those who have come to count on us."

Chapter Ten

Sutherland Keep

Imminent danger? Really? If the Sutherland's wife or child were in any kind of imminent danger, Aila would eat her plaid. And considering she hadn't had more than a few bites of a dried oatcake on the day-long ride it had taken to get here from Borve Castle, she was more than hungry enough to do just that.

Maggie Sutherland was anything but in danger. Other than the occasional completely normal pain, the plump young woman's cheeks glowed with health, her eyes sparkled with mischief, and she spoke at length without having to stop and catch her breath even once.

And the child? On examination of the mam-to-be's quite large, round tummy, the babe was already head down in position ready to be born, eager, and just as healthy as its mother.

What did obviously ail the young woman, however, was the fact their healer had died suddenly of a lung fever during the long, cold winter, and the laird's wife was simply reluctant to deliver her first child without the aid of someone who had at least a little medical knowledge.

And who could blame her?

Though this was 1643 and a more progressive time, the number of women who still succumbed to one complication or another of childbirth was truly frightening.

Aila sighed.

Even with the threat Fergus had made hanging over her head, what wouldn't she give to be with a child of her own right now? She'd helped bring many a bairn into the world, all of them kicking and screaming and thankfully turning from that scary blue color they always started out with to a nice healthy pink in a matter of a few breaths.

Despite Fergus, there'd be no chance she'd ever hold a child of her own. For if last night had taught her anything, it was she'd been right all along about her husband. Ian Mackay truly and without a doubt was a *sidhe*, and *sidhe*s weren't capable of fathering children.

And being a *sidhe* was the only explanation that made any sense.

Her husband, this Ian Mackay, was attentive and kind, and oh-so loving. The things he'd done to her body the night before, to her very soul, had her cheeks burning, her palms sweating, the place between her thighs tingling, and her heart pounding. While the Ian Mackay she'd seen lying on the floor, dead in a pool of his own vomit, had not even bothered to look her way one single time before his demise.

This Ian worked just as long and just as hard as his men, and he'd even encouraged her to use her skills ta help their people. The other Ian had been a self-indulgent spoiled tyrant and would never have lifted a hand to do menial labor, let alone allow his wife to touch the sick, in fear he might himself become ill.

And this Ian had given her control of their lovemaking. What a gift that had been. From what Aila had witnessed before his death, the other Ian had been arrogant, rough, and demanding with the serving girls, so his wife's pleasure was something that would never have crossed his mind.

Was it a fair trade off, though? Having her wonderful, magical Ian instead of the awful man whose place he'd somehow taken? Having a kind, loving husband who happened to be fae, instead of a drunken, human brute? Even if it meant they'd never have bairns of their own?

Yes, it was worth it.

It had to be, didn't it?

It was what it was and much too late to change anything about it now.

That didn't mean watching another woman about to become a mother didn't hurt to her very core. To take her mind off her own sadness, Aila forced her healer side to take over. She stoked the fire and tossed a hand full of rosemary and thyme upon it before adding a pinch of cloves to a steaming kettle. It was one of the things Margot had always done when preparing to deliver a babe.

The old woman's voice rang once more in her memory. "The secret ta a successful birthing is all in what ye do beforehand, lass."

Aila could once more see her teacher's kind, wrinkled, old face. "Frist ye dip yer hands, all the way up ta yer elbows, mind ye, in a mixture of lye soap and hot water ta make sure nae fae spirts lingering aboot have attached themselves ta yer fingers," she'd say. "Then sprinkle a dash of cloves in the water fer good measure and luck, 'cause everybody kens fae can nae stand ta be anywhere near cloves."

Her voice would drop to not much more than a

whisper as if she were about to impart a closely guarded secret. "Then scrub them hands hard just as if ye were doing yer laird's laundry, 'cause ye can nae go wrong with a good covering of cloves and lye. And if'n ye do it right, the fae'll stay as far away as they can and nae get the chance ta steal the babe's soul before it has a chance ta draw its first breath."

That's when old Margot would always chuckle. "Then crush up a good hand full of rosemary and thyme and sprinkle them upon the fire just like I taught ye. The smoke will ward off any other evil spirts that may be lingering aboot, looking ta do mischief. Ye do this every time a babe is aboot ta come inta the world, and ye'll see. I'm telling ye, I've nae lost a mither ta childbirth fever since me own dear departed grandmir told me ta do what I'm passing on ta ye now."

Aila smiled. Margot had been right, she hadn't personally lost a mother to the fever that had taken her own mam in at least three years. And since she'd added her own remedy of coriander and honey tea to her regimen, she hadn't lost one ta bleeding either.

****

Sutherland Keep

"Come with me," he pleaded once more.

Ian stood before Aila in the hall's wide-open great room with a half-wilted bunch of heather clutched tightly between his sweaty palms. She'd only been gone from him for three days, yet it had seemed like an eternity. When had his wife become so important to his very existence that he couldn't seem to draw a decent breath if she wasn't sharing the same air? It'd been all Ian could do to let her leave Borve Castle without him. Let alone watch her ride off with a Sutherland, even if it had proven to be an almost pleasant version of one.

But in the end, that was exactly what he had done. What other choice could he have made? He'd seen how desperate the man was about his wife's condition and the coming of their child. And Ian had seen with his own eyes how competent a healer Aila was. If the situation were reversed and it had been Aila who'd needed the help, wouldn't he have done the same? Even if it meant riding right up to his enemy's doorstep.

"I want ta go. I truly do, Ian." Aila sighed. "I've nae ever been ta Inverness. But Maggie's running a slight fever, and the bairn has nae yet figured out how ta latch on ta the teet as tightly as he should. It would nae be wise fer me ta leave them so soon."

He knew she was right, but knowing and accepting the fact that he had to travel to Inverness without her was two different things.

"What if I wait another day or so before the men and I leave," he asked. "Do you think Sutherland's wife and child will be well enough to be left on their own by then?"

She sighed once more and shook her head. "In good conscience, I do nae think so. And I can nae leave until Maggie is nae longer feverish at all. I doubt that'll happen for a few days yet, mayhap a fortnight or more. 'Tis the way with birthing sometimes."

Then she got a gleam in her eye. "But I would nae send ye so far away without giving ye a good reason ta hurry back, husband. That is, if ye be interested in such a thing."

Ian almost choked as he nodded, not trusting himself to speak.

Interested? Hell yeah, he was interested. As a

matter of fact, if he'd been any more interested, he would've embarrassed them both by lifting her skirts and taking her right then and there up against the hard, stone wall.

But the problem was, they weren't at Borve castle and this wasn't their home. This was a Sutherland keep, a potential enemy stronghold, and he'd best not forget it. Not to mention the fact he'd barely found his way to the livery earlier, let alone an empty bedroom where he could take his fill of his wife.

It was as if Aila could read his mind as she pointed to the bunch of heather he still clutched tightly in his hand.

"Where did ye pick that?" she whispered.

Ian gulped. "Down by the loch."

Then he thrust them toward her so forcibly she almost lost her balance trying to catch them. But she didn't, and she grinned, giggled, and turned on her heel as she crocked a finger in his direction. "I believe both Maggie and the bairn are sleeping and will be for a while, so how aboot we go down ta that loch and see if we can find some more."

There actually was quite a bit more heather scattered all about, but neither one of them gave it any more than a passing glance. They were too busy removing each other's garments.

When he finally had her naked and standing before him, Ian grinned as he pulled her close and nuzzled her neck. "I've missed you something fierce."

Aila sighed and leaned in even closer. "I've missed ye, too, *sidhe*, though it's only been a few days. I fear I've grown much too used ta yer face and the sound of yer voice, let alone the feel of ye deep inside me."

Ian growled low and deep, and the sound made Aila giggle as he slowly led her toward the water. "You think me some kind of magical creature now. Let's see what you think once I'm done," he whispered.

She pulled out of his grasp. "Have ye lost yer mind, then? I'm nae getting in that water. I do nae ken how ta swim, and Scot water is always too cold." She waved her arms about. "And, and, and we have a right fine meadow all around us, ye ken. And it's warm."

He chuckled as he grabbed her up into his arms, and she squealed as he headed into the loch anyway. "I'm magic, remember?" he whispered against the soft skin of her neck. "I'll keep you warm and safe, Aila. For I mean to have you wet and wanting today wife, and I'll settle for nothing else."

She sighed, shivered, and clung to his neck tighter as chilly water splashed up her legs and wrapped itself about her waist.

With no more than the touch of his chin against hers, Ian had Aila's full attention. "Trust me in this, please. I won't let any harm come to you. I promise." Then he captured her lips with his and sealed his promise with a kiss.

At first, she was a little hesitant. Still, she tasted of home and family, everything good, everything right and familiar in his world mixed with just a dab of her rebellious nature, and Ian gloried in it.

Then she relaxed in his arms and kissed him back so fervently he almost lost his balance.

Water splashed up and wet their torsos, and Ian shivered. Aila was right. This water was quite chilly, but the contrast of the cold water and their hot slick skin sliding against each other was more than worth it.

He broke their kiss, and lifting Aila's legs up along his hips, he entered her in one swift movement. She gasped once, then twice, before instinctively wrapping her legs snuggly about his waist.

"I've nae ever heard of such a thing." She giggled.

Ian growled low and deep as he increased the power of his thrusts. "I've dreamed of taking you this way more times than I can remember."

She leaned back in his arms and grinned. "It's a lucky woman who has a *sidhe* for a husband I am thinking."

He heard her words. He really did, but the sight before him had him mesmerized. Aila laid bare, her brilliant red hair floating upon the water, her rich raspberry-colored nipples all puckered and wet. He couldn't resist. He simply had to have a taste.

And what a taste it was.

The sensation of her pebbly hard flesh against his lips mixed with her natural sweetness upon his tongue had his cock quickly spasming out of control at the same time she locked her legs ever tighter about his waist and shouted her release.

They just stood there a few minutes, not saying a word but simply catching their breath. It wasn't until Ian was carrying Aila back toward the shore that he noticed he wasn't the least bit cold anymore.

Still, it was a sunny spot he chose to lay out his plaid to make them a bed. He pulled her into his arms and rubbed his warmth into her.

She sighed as she snuggled in closer and closed her eyes. "I'm going to miss ye something fierce when ye are gone, Ian. It seems I've come to care much too much for ye. I may even love ye, I'm thinking. I should have guarded me heart better."

"I'll be back before you know it," he whispered back.

"Aye, I ken you will this time, but I mean ye will leave me fer good one day." She once again sighed. "*Sidhes* do nae ever stay anywhere fer long, ye ken? They can nae. It's the way of magical creatures."

He wanted to argue with her. He wanted to once more tell her he wasn't a fucking fairy, but then what good would that do? He did plan on leaving her, didn't he? Danny and his men were waiting to be saved. He'd made a deal with Fate. So, instead of telling her that he was beyond any doubt in love with her, too, and that he really wasn't a fucking fairy for the thousandth time, he simply lay his head close to hers and asked, "Is there anything I can bring you back from Inverness, anything you want or need?"

She kissed his cheek and shook her head. "Just ye, Ian. Bring yerself back ta me. That's all I need."

****

Inverness wasn't anything like Ian expected.

Not that he'd had a clue what to expect in the first place. Especially considering where he'd been and what he'd been doing since first awakening in the seventeenth century. The closest he'd come to seeing anything he'd call city-like before today was when he'd looked up from the field last week and noticed a cloud that reminded him of the state of New York, complete with what appeared to be the Statue of Liberty hanging off to one side.

Did traveling back through time rattle one's brain?

Perhaps it did a little, but while Inverness could technically be described as a city, it was certainly not like any city he'd ever seen. Streets of simple cobblestone stretched on and on while people and animals alike roamed about, not really going anywhere, but always in motion. A stone church sat right alongside a thatched cottage while a real frigging castle could be seen perched atop a distant hill. They were surrounded on all sides by row after row of open air market stalls, all huddled closely together and overflowing with all manner of goods, like fresh breads, roasted meats, vegetables, and sweet-treats being hawked by very loud vendors.

Ian's mouth watered, and his stomach grumbled. The long-ago breakfast of dried oatcakes and stale ale hadn't in the least been satisfying.

He shook off his hunger and forced himself to concentrate on the task at hand. There would be plenty of time later to contemplate his body's desire to be fed, but first, he had to do what he'd come for and see to his people's needs.

His fingers itched to spend the precious coins hidden deep within his sporran as the tables he'd been searching for came into sight. Baskets of grains, both barley and oats, covered the first one, and all he could think was, thank god, it wasn't fucking corn. There were the pens filled with scrawny chickens and pudgy little piglets. Next to the pens was a table covered with various swords and knives and another loaded down with herbs of every variety.

Ian chuckled as he realized he was more excited today about this shopping trip than he'd been at the age of fifteen when his parents had taken him to The Mall of America in Minnesota. The smell of human and animal waste and sweat permeated the air, but he wouldn't trade this small market place in Inverness for the vastness of that modern one.

His only regret was he really had no idea how to go about bartering for what he wanted, because not only did the memories of the previous Ian Mackay prove useless, but he hadn't bothered to pay attention when his twenty-first century history teacher had been lecturing on the subject. But then history hadn't been one of his strong points, either, and especially not fucking Scottish history.

He couldn't remember if he'd ever taken a European Studies class. If he had, to his way of thinking, it'd probably ranked right up there with growing corn and slopping hogs so he hadn't paid any more attention than he'd had to.

Back then, his interests had been more along the athletic lines, like football, track, chasing after girls, and trying to keep up with his good friend Danny. He'd graduated at the top of his class, but it wasn't because of any grade he'd ever earned in a history class.

Or a geography class either, for that matter. Until just a few hours ago, he hadn't known the real-life Loch Ness he always heard about, along with its supposed elusive resident, was right outside Inverness.

Ian chuckled. Had the famous monster so many tourists spent hours searching for even been born yet…if it did exist. If it had, perhaps he'd get a chance to catch a glimpse of baby Nessie on his way out of town.

Wouldn't that be something?

But as of right now, he had more important matters to contemplate, and he wished desperately he would've paid more attention, not only in history and geography class but also to what his dad had tried to teach him about farming. People were counting on him to make the right choices today and to buy what was needed…and so was Aila.

A dull ache filled his chest and caught Ian by surprise. God, how he missed her and the touch of her lips upon his, and her laugh and her smile, and the feel of her warm welcoming body beneath his.

His cock hardened, and he hoped desperately that his pretty little wife would be ready to return home with him when this shopping trip was over.

With a smile, Ian stepped up to the nearest market stall and fingered the coins in his sporran. He might not be the most experienced highlander when it came to bargaining, but he'd give it his best shot. For he had a sudden overwhelming urge to get this shopping trip over with, collect Aila Mackay, and take her sweet little ass home.

His cock hardened even further in response to his thoughts.

Chapter Eleven

End of June 1643
Sutherland Keep

Ian held the basket out toward her and grinned. "Are you ready to come home now?"

Aila glanced at the contents and gasped. "I do nae understand, Ian."

He'd brought her herbs. And not just any herbs, but milk thistle among other things.

What highland warrior knew what any given herb was used for, let alone which ones to purchase? But he had. Precious eucalyptus, mugwort, roseroot, bearberry, and bogbean. All the ones she'd been dangerously low on.

He chuckled. "I know you said you didn't want anything from Inverness, but I didn't want to return empty handed. I wanted to bring you something you'd like, and I know how much you need all of those. How much our people need them. You know, just something simple, like the eucalyptus for Daniel's cough and the milk thistle for stomach issues."

She was astonished. Not only did he know their uses, but he was so obviously proud of himself for bringing her back something he knew she needed, something he knew would put a smile on her face. As if he really did care.

Aila chocked back the tears threatening to close her

throat. "Were ye able ta find everything ye were looking fer then and had coin left over?"

He nodded. "Yes, I found everything we need and then some. I even spent three shillings on whisky to celebrate with the men. And I got chickens and pigs to boot."

Now she knew something was wrong, very wrong. He'd spent three whole shillings just on whisky for himself and his men without bartering down the price? If there was one fact about a Scot all could agree upon, it was they tightened the drawstrings of their purses so taut not even a whiff of air dare accost their precious coin.

And though she was surprised he'd spent so much good coin on whisky and medicinal herbs, she'd never understand why any highlander would part with even a farthing for chickens and pigs of all things instead of knives and claymores, which he hadn't mentioned one word about. Especially since they had a perfectly good ocean not far away and it was chock full of fish. Let alone the red-tailed dear in abundance.

"I'm going to build a right proper chicken coup and hog house," he went on excitedly. "Before you know it, we'll have eggs aplenty, not to mention hams and bacon. They'll provide the variety we need to keep our people healthy. You know, by adding extra protein to our diet."

All she could do was stare. Who in their right mind, if not controlled by fae, wasted time building anything for a chicken to live in, let alone a pig?

It wasn't as if their people penned up the sheep. Why would you bother with chickens or pigs?

And protein?

What was protein?

She'd never heard such nonsense.

****

July 1643

Borve Castle

What the hell was wrong with his brain?

He should be training his men how to defend themselves and their land better. At best, he probably had no more than a handful of highlanders who even knew one end of a claymore from another, let alone how to swing one. Sadly, young Daniel was probably one of his very best.

He should have been clearing yet another field for planting, even though that would probably piss off Amos. The stubborn old farmer didn't seem to appreciate his opinion or interference when it came to the fields. Not that Ian really cared what the crotchety old man thought. If Ian said the sky was blue, then Amos Mackay would swear it was green.

He should have been seeing to the stupid chickens and hogs. At the very least, he should have been checking with Old Brody as to when the fishing boat could go out again since they were all done with the drying and processing of last week's catch.

But was he doing any of those things?

Nope, he sure wasn't.

Ian stared up at the silhouette of his wife through the open shutters of the castle's only tower and sighed. He truly was head-over-heals in love with Aila, and though he knew it wasn't fair to either one of them, he couldn't seem to help himself. Not only was she beautiful, but she was smart and funny and generous with their people and caring and talented and so many other things he wasn't.

To make matters worse, he couldn't seem to keep his hands and other body parts off her whenever she was anywhere near. That was the real problem, because he had no idea how long he'd be here in the past.

Tobias Moiré could show up anytime now.

He'd married the woman just as he'd been instructed to do. He'd rebuilt the castle, for the most part anyway. He'd put into action a solution to the food problem for these people in his charge, and he'd even made peace with at least one faction of Sutherlands. So it was definitely possible Fate could appear any day now and tell him it was time to go.

Could he just walk away now, especially knowing the future of his friend and his men hung in the balance? He wasn't so sure that he could.

Then again, would he be able to live with himself if he left Aila all alone here in 1643 and possibly pregnant with his child?

Well, technically, if she were to get pregnant, it wouldn't be his child. It would biologically belong to the original Ian Mackay. It would be the other man's offspring. Still, it didn't feel right. Like it or not, a child being produced would still be because of his actions.

And though Aila was convinced he was some kind of fucking fairy and couldn't possibly father a child, Ian was pretty sure he could. Even if he was using another man's dick to do it. At the very least, since there was no such thing as modern birth control in this time period, he was certainly risking it every single chance he got. His little wife was so damn receptive to his attention, who could blame him?

He smiled as the memory of the night before

flooded his mind. Aila naked and wanting, her long red curls tickling his chest as she rode him fast and hard. Aila whispering soft words of endearment against his neck while begging him to end her torment. Aila finally screaming her release as she tightened around his cock and he coated her insides with his cum. And the sight of Aila falling asleep in his arms, tucked up close to his heart.

How could he ever give that up?

It wasn't just how receptive she was to him in bed either.

The way she'd looked at him when he handed her the stupid milk thistle bouquet had almost dropped him to his knees. Her eyes had misted over with unshed tears, and her lips had trembled as she broke out into a smile so bright it was almost blinding.

He'd felt like a king, like the luckiest of men, and all because he'd given a pretty girl a silly bunch of weeds and she'd liked it.

But then he'd known she would. He'd watched her treat their people often enough. Growing up in an Amish community, it'd been impossible to not learn at least the very basics of herbology, even if he hadn't wanted to. Though, he was glad now that he had.

Like the eucalyptus. She'd almost creamed her panties when he handed her the small pouch of herbs he'd seen her use on Daniel in the same way his own mother had when hay fever made his breathing difficult.

Ian's lips lifted into a smile he couldn't seem to suppress. Aila didn't wear panties. Nobody did. A little tidbit of information about life in 1643 Scotland he wouldn't be sharing with Fate or anyone else anytime soon.

And the mugwort... She'd been astonished he'd known simple mugwort was used for intestinal problems like diarrhea and worms, as well as a liver tonic. But she'd lost her smile when he'd later informed her that mugwort was used for menstrual problems, too. She'd turned so pale he'd been afraid she was about to pass out. Apparently, men in 1643 didn't speak about woman's cycles, ever, and especially not to a woman.

No wonder she thought him to be a fucking fairy.

It was something he was going to have to remember not to do again.

After the mugwort, he hadn't gone into detail about the roseroot, bearberry, or the bogbean. He'd simply told her that the person selling them had told him they were good for nerves and festerings and achy joints and such. She'd kind of taken him at his word. Or at least she hadn't questioned him further, and he was thankful for that.

****

Perhaps she should make herself a tonic.

Aila was so tired today, and if she didn't know better, she'd swear she was falling even deeper in love with her husband. That she simply couldn't afford to do. It was dangerous to develop feelings for a highlander laird let alone one who was also a *sidhe*. But the symptoms of her foolishness were all around her. Her heart sped up every time he walked into the room, her skin immediately heated to an almost uncomfortable warmth whenever he touched her, and just the sight of his smile made her feel as if she might swoon.

It was ridiculous.

Her eyes misted at the memory of him bringing her a hand full of milk thistle when he'd returned and collected her from Sutherland lands. Who in their right mind cried over milk thistle of all things?

It simply wasn't acceptable.

Oh no, one didn't dare fall in love with a *sidhe* without dire consequences. The fae weren't known for sharing the affections of those they possessed. Everyone knew that, so they were obviously responsible for her tiredness and her sickness. They were trying to confuse her mind.

Aila yawned, glanced toward the small pallet on the floor before her holding her latest patient, and longed for just a short little nap. Perhaps an hourglass or two of rest and she'd be able to shed herself of these silly romantic feelings for Ian, and the fae would leave her alone once more.

But then tiredness and lack of clear thinking had been Aila's chief complaint since she'd returned home from helping with the birthing of Laird Stephen Sutherland's heir more than a sennight ago. Tiredness and the fact she couldn't seem to keep her food down and her bleeding time was later than usual. If she didn't know better and if she wasn't sure the fae were involved, she'd swear she was with child.

But that couldn't be the case, could it?

There had to be another explanation. For when Ian returned from Inverness, he'd proven beyond any shadow of a doubt once more that he truly was a *sidhe*.

Oh yes, the fae were trying to confuse her because she was falling in love with her husband.

It wasn't entirely her fault though. He smiled her way every time they were anywhere close to each other, even at the risk of ignoring his men. He spoke to her as if she were his equal instead of his wife, even though most of the time she had no clue what he was talking about.

And the nights? Oh my god, the nights.

She smiled.

Every night he tupped her silly, holding her tenderly, stroking her, caressing her, kissing her, rocking her ta sleep from the inside out. Though there were times he'd wake with a start, troubled by something he refused to share. During those times, he'd quickly leave her side without a single word as to why.

Where did he go when he slipped from their bed in the middle of the night? Did he go in search of the fae who possessed him?

There'd been many times she'd been tempted to follow and find out.

If it wasn't the fae he was looking for, could it be another woman? After all, it was common practice for men to keep mistresses. It was their god given right after all.

God given right or not, her husband had better not be seeking comfort in another woman's arms while she herself was tired all the time and retching each morning just because the fae didn't wish to share him with her. And if the fae weren't willing to share Ian with her, then she certainly wasn't going to share him with anyone else either.

The scorch of jealousy filled her to overflowing, and Aila's fingers itched to rip the hair right out of the head of any lass bold enough to dare look her man's way. *Sidhe* or nae, possessed by the fae or nae, he was still her husband and hers alone.

Still, the fact remained, even discounting the fae's influence, something was wrong with her that she simply couldn't explain. Since it wasn't possible she could be with child, then what could it be? Sadly, she was the only healer for miles around, so there wasn't anyone she could ask.

Damn Ian Mackay's sexy, bonny hide for being a *sidhe* and not a mortal man. For who knew how long the fae would make her ill because of her desire for him.

Aila sighed. "Ye are still just a wean and need ta stay on yer pallet at night and nae be out wandering around the countryside looking for trouble."

She tried her best to keep a stern look on her face, but it was hard with Daniel glancing up at her with tears misting his eyes. "If'n ye would, ye would nae be tripping over yer own two feet in the dark and cutting yer arm in the first place."

She wrapped a strip of linen around said arm and tied it off.

Daniel sniffed once and swiped at his eyes with his uninjured hand, leaving a streak of dirt all the way across his small face. "The laird knows I keep look-out for Sutherlands." He stuck out his chin, and for just a moment it trembled. "He counts on me, Ian Mackay does, and I'll nae be letting him down."

She placed her hands on her hips and tried to reason with the child once more. "Well, ye will nae be much use ta the laird if ye bleed ta death in the middle of the night where no one can find ye, now will ye?"

Agnes the cook coughed somewhere in the distance, and it distracted her from her lecture to Daniel. She knew it was Cook, because since the very first day the old woman had come to the castle to take up her duties, it was what she always did to get Aila's attention.

What could it be this time?

Were the kitchen lasses not moving fast enough to suit her again? Or was the larder missing some ingredient she simply had to have in order to make whatever dish she deemed important for this particular evening's meal? Or was the peat boy not yet back from collecting the fuel for the day's fires? Or any of a number of other complaints Cook made on a regular basis.

Aila sighed once more.

It was still quite early in the morning, the sun not yet fully up, yet she had already treated a runny nose, a cranky highlander with a hangover, a colicky baby, its overly tired mother, and three minor sword wounds from Ian's training of his men this day. And those had all been before young Daniel had shown up with a gash in his arm from a stumble he'd taken.

God, she was tired and wished that just this once she could forget about this castle, these people, her duties, and even Ian as far as that went. All she wanted this very moment was to go back to bed. Her stomach threatened to heave even though she hadn't so much as taken a sip of tea for fear it would come right back up. But then perhaps tea was exactly what she needed. A soothing mint perhaps, or a chamomile would be nice.

Aila had almost forgotten about Cook when the woman coughed again. She chuckled softly to herself as she turned toward the sound. It appeared tea and a nap would have to wait until the duties of the lady of the castle had been fulfilled.

The chubby older woman with hair as white as snow, face red as a beet from the kitchen fires, and an apron well saturated with grease stains crooked a finger in her direction.

Aila followed. She'd learned in her first sennight here it was easier to simply remain quiet and listen to what these people thought best before ever offering her opinion. Much like the Gordon clan she'd been born into, or the Sutherlands for that matter.

She chuckled again. Perhaps it was more a Scottish trait to always have something to say about everything, instead of it being a particular clan one.

They'd no sooner stepped from the great hall to a small private alcove when Agnes came right to the point. "I'd think, since it's obvious ta any with eyes ye are now carrying yerself, ye'd be gentler with the wean. Young Daniel means well, ye ken? It's nae his fault he goes out each night searching fer Sutherlands. He was nae more than an arm's length away from the old laird when the murder happened, and he's made hisself a vow ta never let anything like that happen again on his watch. He's an honorable lad, that one. Leave him ta do what he feels needs doing."

The old woman rattled on and on, but Aila had stopped listening after the "it's obvious ta any with eyes ye are now carrying yerself," comment. It couldn't be true. It simply couldn't be. Could it? *Sidhe*s could nae father children. And if she was carrying a babe, then Ian Mackay was nae more a *sidhe* than she was.

Heat filled her cheeks as it made its way to the very roots of her hair. Her breath came in quick little gasps, and the room began to spin a heartbeat before everything went completely black.

Chapter Twelve

"Aila, wake up, lass," Ian shouted. Panic filled him as he gently shook her shoulder once more.

What the hell was wrong with his wife? The cook hadn't told him anything except that one moment Aila had been fine and the next she'd been passed out cold on the floor. He'd carried her to their room, laid her gently upon their furs, and then he'd shut out the gawking keep staff so they wouldn't see how incompetent their laird really was.

In Afghanistan, he'd had medics to handle this kind of stuff. In Ohio, he'd had his mom. But this wasn't Afghanistan, and it sure-as-hell wasn't Ohio.

What options did he have available to him?

What if no matter what he did, she still didn't wake?

Ian shook his head. No, he wouldn't think like that and he wouldn't panic, at least not yet.

In the war, he'd seen many men die right before his eyes from every possible scenario he could think of, such as gunshot wounds, dysentery, mortar attacks, roadside bombs, and simply not paying attention to their surroundings, but they were soldiers, for the most part anyway, and they sure as hell weren't Aila.

She was so pale, so very, very pale, and cooler to the touch than he thought she should be. Had someone poisoned her because she'd once been a member of the

Sutherland clan? After all, did he really know any of these people? Especially the cook, Agnes. Could anyone ever really trust the cook? In every murder mystery he'd ever watched, it had always been the butler or the cook who committed the crime, and at Castle Borve, they didn't have a butler.

He leaned in close and sniffed at Aila's shallow breath but couldn't detect anything other than her normal sweet scent.

His heart skipped a beat, and his breath caught in his chest. She'd wake. She was his wife and the woman who completely owned his heart. Of course, she'd wake. She simply had to. If she didn't, he was going to kill himself a cook, even if Agnes had always come across as the sweet, little old lady type.

He shook Aila again, a little harder this time.

But what if she didn't wake?

What would he do?

After all, who else could he even ask for help? She was the healer, the only healer in the whole northern section of this God forsaken, frigging country. She simply had to wake up, and now.

Panic threatened to close off his throat to the point he could barely draw a breath. His forehead broke out into a sheen of sweat that matched his palms. His legs felt weak, and his sweaty hands began to tremble.

Then a miracle happened.

Slowly, her eyelids flickered open and her gaze cleared.

It was on the tip of his tongue to shout his relief for all the world to hear when his wife balled up her cute, tiny, little fist and punched him square in the nose, hard.

"Liar," she yelled.

Ian jumped back out of her reach.

"Ye are a liar, Ian Mackay, and I'll nae forgive ye for it as long as I live. I swear I'll nae. Ye are nae more a *sidhe* than I."

For a moment, he was stumped. What the hell was she talking about? Then his shock turned to anger. "I've never once said I was a *sidhe*. As a matter of fact, if I remember correctly, I've told you all along that I'm not. You're the one who keeps insisting I'm some kind of fucking fairy, not me."

It was more than obvious that Aila was way past the point of being spitting mad when she hissed her response right back at him.

"Ye may nae have admitted it out loud, but ye ken good and well I had me reasons ta believe ye were. Ye tricked me, husband, and well ye ken it. And since ye are obviously nae a *sidhe*, ye'll be explaining ta me why ye are so different from the Ian Mackay I first saw, and ye'll be explaining it ta me right now. I'll be having the truth this time, and don't think I'll nae, or I'll be a shouting my concerns about ye loud and clear for all ta hear. We'll just see what happens ta yer sorry arse then."

Ian ran his fingers through his hair. On one hand, he was glad his wife no longer considered him a fucking fairy, but on the other, how was he going to explain something even more unbelievable. It wasn't as if he could simply blurt out the fact that he was from almost four hundred years in the future and a completely different body to boot. Could he?

No, he couldn't.

When he'd been unceremoniously dumped into Laird Ian Mackay's body, he hadn't known much about the time period or the country, but he'd always been a fast learner, and two things had become abundantly clear early on about highlanders. Scots were extremely superstitious and crazy religious. If he didn't play his cards right, he could very well end up accused of witchcraft, tied to a stake, and set on fire before he even knew what was happening.

He shuddered.

Becoming a human toasted marshmallow wasn't appealing in the least and wouldn't go very far in completing his assigned task and getting the opportunity to get back his lost friend and squad members either. So that meant coming up with a feasible reason for not being the dead man his wife was sure she'd seen.

But what?

He needed time to come up with a believable scenario, so he did the only thing he could think of, he stalled. "What happened to make you change your mind about me being possessed by the fairies?"

She crossed her arms and glared at him. "As I've told ye before, *sidhe*s can nae father bairns, Ian."

For a split second, he didn't understand, then comprehension smacked him square in the face and he reeled from it. "I'm going to be a father? We…we…we are going to have a baby?"

He couldn't help himself, he grinned.

She nodded slowly. "Aye, that is if ye happen ta live long enough ta actually become one."

The gleam in her eye reminded Ian of his mom on the rare occasions she'd been miffed with his dad, and it brought to mind a piece of advice his father had once given him.

"When you find yourself on the wrong side of a woman's ire, son, just start quoting scriptures. It'll not only throw them off guard, but nine times outta ten, if you do it right, it might even make them forget what they were so mad at you about in the first place. And trust me, it never hurts to ask for a little divine intervention when dealing with an angry female. If you ask me, the whole darn species tends to be vicious when riled."

He cleared his throat, thankful for all those Sunday sermons he hadn't really wanted to attend in the first place. "He cried with a loud voice," Ian boomed. "Lazarus come forth! And he who had been dead came out bound hand and foot with graveclothes, and his face was wrapped with a cloth. Jesus said to them, 'Loose him, and let him go.'"

Confusion crossed Aila's face. She looked as if she were about to speak, but he wasn't going to give her that chance. At least not yet.

"Yeah though I walk through the valley of the shadow of death I shall fear no evil. Thy rod and thy staff they comfort me."

Aila held up a hand. "Cease. What are ye prattling on aboot, husband? Ye are making nae sense at all."

Ian shrugged. "I'm trying to explain why I'm so different now from the man you remember me to be."

He almost chuckled. Aila really did look confused. A crease formed between her eyes. Her gaze seemed to be trying to penetrate his soul, and deep frown lines graced both sides of her mouth.

He didn't chuckle, however. That would've defeated the whole purpose. Because if it was a story she wanted, then it was a story she'd get, thanks to a technique he'd learned in Escape and Evasion classes his first year of Marine training. In other words, stick as close to the truth as possible without giving away any useful information. All the while not giving one's interrogator the opportunity to really question one in return.

Again, she started to open her mouth to speak, but he beat her to it. "You see, I've often wondered if you were right, and I did come very close to actually dying that night."

He sighed long and loud for effect. "I remember going up the stairs, and I remember going into my room, but after that, I don't remember much of anything until I woke up sometime in the middle of the night coughing and sputtering and choking on something vile. I've never been so cold in my entire life. And I hurt everywhere—my head, my stomach, my arms, my legs, and even the roots of my fucking hair."

Ian paused for effect and took one of Aila's hands in his and held on tight. For the life of him, he couldn't bring himself to look her in the eye.

"I think I really would've lost my life that night if it hadn't been for you and God. I believe that, somewhere in the back of my mind, I heard you call my name. And I knew that very moment, I wanted to live if for nothing more than to keep my promise to you and to our king of course.

"In my stupor, I begged God for a second chance, you see, and I believe he heard my prayer. I promised him that if he'd let me live, I'd change my evil ways. I'd stop whoring and drinking to excess and thinking only of myself. I'd be a better man, a good husband to you and a good laird to our people. And when I woke, everything about me was changed."

Aila's eyes misted over with tears. "Truly, Ian? Ye were nae dead? Or possessed by the fae?"

He felt like the biggest jerk in the whole wide world. She looked so trusting, so innocent, so precious. Granted, not everything he'd said to her had been a complete lie. After all, he really had woken up coughing and sputtering, but just in someone else's body. His head had really pounded like the dickens. And he had been sent back to life by a heavenly creature, though no one in their right mind would ever consider Tobias Moiré, better known as Fate, as being even remotely god-like.

But he didn't say any of that to Aila. Instead he wrapped her in his arms, brought her up against his warm hard body, and whispered close to her ear, "No, I wasn't dead, I promise. And the only thing I've ever been possessed by is you."

****

He thought her a fool.

Aila stood at the window of her chamber looking down upon the courtyard below, watching Ian as he went from one clansman to another discussing whatever important matters men discussed with each other, and her very soul hurt.

He obviously thought her a fool and not worthy of his trust or the truth. Just as every other man she'd known. Just as her brother had. And what made it even worse was, she'd really begun to think Ian was different.

It wasn't fair. It wasn't right. But she knew it to be the plight of being born female, and like it or not, she'd best get used to it. Or at least that's what she'd always been told. Men do not converse with women. Men fuck women when the desire strikes them, they eat food women cook, they wear garments women sew, and they put babes in a woman's belly every chance they get, but they do not share anything resembling the truth of whatever they think or do with such a lowly creature as a lass.

She stomped her foot, and her anger rose.

She didn't wish to get used to being lied to and ignored like so many other women did. She'd hoped Ian would grow to trust her as more than just the lass who warmed his bed. That he'd see her for what she truly could be—an ally, a confidant, a partner. Even when she'd thought him to be a *sidhe*, she'd wanted it to be so and feared it would never be. And now that she knew he wasn't possessed by the fae, she was even more convinced the situation was hopeless.

"I think I really would've lost my life that night if it hadn't been for you and God," he'd said. "I believe that somewhere in the back of my mind I heard you call my name. And I knew that very moment, I wanted to live if for nothing more than to keep my promise to you, and to our king of course."

Ha!

Even if she hadn't always had an uncanny ability to know a lie when she heard one, she would've known that to be untrue. Ian Mackay hadn't heard the sound of her voice before his untimely demise because she hadn't spoken to him before saying her vows that next morning, let alone him giving two hoots about any promises he'd made anybody.

"In my stupor, I begged God for a second chance, and I believe he heard my prayer. I promised him I'd change my evil ways."

Double ha!

He hadn't even been able to look her straight in the eye when he told those bald-faced lies. Did he think her stupid? Or simply slow witted? Or so pathetic she'd believe anything he had to say just because the words flowed from his mouth like honey?

Well, she didn't believe him. Not even for the space of time it took for one single grain of sand to drop through the hourglass.

But the fact remained, something had happened that night. After all, she was with child and since she hadn't lain with any man but Ian, he couldn't be a *sidhe*. And since he was not a *sidhe*, then what powers had been at work in that room? Because since Ian Mackay still breathed and walked and talked and did everything else every other man did the morning after his demise, then some power of some kind, even if it wasn't fae, had taken control of the situation. The only question left was, was the power one of good or evil, and how was she to ascertain which?

"No, I wasn't dead, I promise," he'd whispered so sweetly. "And the only thing I've ever been possessed by is you."

Triple ha!

She shook her head and glared down at her lying husband. He thought himself so smart. But if there was one thing she knew beyond any shadow of a doubt, it was what a dead man looked like. She'd seen death on enough faces in her lifetime to know. And Ian Mackay had been, without a doubt, stone-cold dead, no matter what excuse he came up with now. Dead was dead. Always had been and always would be. The dead did not simply come back to life whenever they wished. At least not without a damn good explanation. Ian Mackay's explanation had been anything but good.

So, the only question remaining was, what was she going to do about it?

For the first time in hours, Aila smiled as her anger bubbled over.

Men might very well think they made the rules, but it was the women who'd perfected ways around every single one of them. Lasses were born understanding men were simple creatures that needed careful guidance. If they hadn't understood that fact of life at birth, then it was a lesson they'd learned early on, at their mam's teets. Though she'd never had a mam of her own to teach her the ways of the world, she'd been raised among strong women who'd been more than willing to impart their knowledge.

Yeah, men made the rules, or at least they thought they did. But one other thing Aila knew was there wasn't much a man wouldn't do to remedy the situation if deprived of his creature comforts, and until Ian Mackay decided to tell her the truth, he was going to find his creature comforts quite few and far between starting this verra day. He might very well run the day-to-day dealings of the clan, but it was she who ran the keep.

Slipping from the chamber she shared with her husband, Aila headed back downstairs. There people to talk to and plans to be made.

Oh yeah, Ian Mackay was, without a doubt, going to regret being an untruthful cad.

****

It took Ian almost an hour to find Aila, and the only

reason he did was because old Agnes took pity upon him and told him where to look. She'd moved every stitch of her belongings to the other side of the castle, to a small chamber that had originally been set up for storage but was now apparently his wife's bedroom. And if the look on her face was any indication, she wasn't the least bit happy that he'd come visiting.

"Is there something ye require, husband?" Her voice was as cold as ice.

Why was she mad? He'd given her a perfectly good explanation of why he wasn't really dead. But apparently his explanation hadn't been good enough, because she stood tapping her foot impatiently and looking as if she wanted to slam the wooden door in his face.

He opened his mouth to speak, but she raised a hand to stop him. "Nae more lies, Ian. Do nae bother ta speak ta me at all until ye can tell me the truth of what happened ta ye."

Again, he started to speak, and she shushed him. "I am nae a fool, and I do nae appreciate being taken for one. Ye begged God," she scoffed. "Ye heard my voice, and ye pleaded ta come back ta me. Ye promised ta change. It's all nonsense." She stomped her foot. "I'll have the truth, or I'll have none ta do with ye from this day forward. Ye'll sleep alone, ye'll eat alone, and ye'll find nae comfort in my arms.

"All I ever asked for was the simple truth. I deserve that much, but ye could nae give it ta me. Well, I demand it now or else."

What was he going to say? He couldn't tell her the truth. There were days he didn't believe it himself. But he had to say something. He couldn't just continue to stand in her doorway, staring at her as if she'd lost her mind.

So he said the first thing that popped in his head. "I've told you the truth, Aila, and if you don't believe me, then I don't know what else to say."

She nodded. "So be it, Ian."

Then she placed her small wide-open palm in the middle of his chest and pushed. Before he even realized what had happened, Ian Mackay found himself staring at Aila's closed door.

Chapter Thirteen

August 1643
Borve Castle

There was no doubt about it, his wife was trying to either starve him to death or drive him completely crazy, and probably both. Well, it wasn't going to work. He'd given her a perfectly reasonable explanation of what had happened the night the original Ian Mackay died, and if she chose to not only not believe him, but to try and punish him every chance she got, then that was her problem, not his.

He slurped another gulp of his tepid, gross, fish broth and glared at the woman responsible.

Aila Mackay, though beautiful, was pure evil at heart. There was no denying that fact. For more than a sennight, his food had been disgusting. His ale sour, his clothing rough and scratchy, his boots wet and muddy, his bed cold and lonely, and any sign of affection completely non-existent. If the sour look on her face this very moment was any indication, she wouldn't be warming up to him anytime soon.

He'd always thought women who were carrying became softer, kinder, more Madonna like. Fuck that, not his wife.

Perhaps he should tell her the truth. It would serve her right. Perhaps he should just shout it from the roof tops and let everyone know he was from almost four hundred years in the future and after his own death had been transported back through time and crammed into the body of one of his distant ancestors. What would she do then when her crazy husband was burned at the stake for witchcraft and she and their child were sent back to a brother who considered her a traitor for doing what her king commanded?

But then he couldn't tell her the truth, now could he? He wouldn't dare.

If she hadn't believed what he already told her, she sure as hell wasn't going to believe what really did happen. And why should she? Hell, there were days Ian wondered if he hadn't simply dreamed up his entire other life before waking in 1643. But there were things impossible to simply dream up. Like the months on end in Iraq and Afghanistan that he'd spent. That Danny had died right before his eyes. That his father had tried in vain to raise him to be a farmer. And that, at the end of his life, he'd almost run down an innocent, little Amish girl with his pickup truck, and all because he was trying to outrun his demons.

No, unfortunately none of it had been a dream. A nightmare at times, for certain, but not a dream.

So what then could he do to make things better between Aila and himself if telling her the truth was out of the question? There had to be something. After all, men all throughout the ages had been successfully navigating their way around angry wives with less information available to them than he possessed.

Then it hit him. Of course, he really was in possession of information that Aila wasn't. Gadgets and gizmos that would astound her. But what could he make and give her fashioned solely out of materials found in

1643? It wasn't as if he had batteries at his disposal, let alone wires, nuts, bolts, or screws.

Something simple perhaps?

Something personal?

Something that, if found three hundred years from now, wouldn't mess with the time-space continuum or whatever time travel crap had been called in the sci-fi movies he used to watch on TV.

Did he even need to worry about such a thing? The time-space continuum, that was. Should he ask Fate before he tried making something from the twenty-first century? And was it even in his power to do something, anything, that might actually alter history? Was there perhaps a fail-safe built into time? Something that would prevent him from succeeding?

He really did need to have a chat with Fate.

****

It wasn't working, and she'd been a fool to think it would.

Aila scrubbed at her teeth with a well-worn stick of wood and sighed. She'd thought by now Ian would've broken down and told her the truth. She thought he would've missed her enough that he wouldn't have been able to resist.

But he hadn't.

Not one single word of a truthful explanation.

She tossed her teeth cleaner to the side and picked up her brush.

It's not as if she wouldn't have known the truth if he'd told it to her, for she would've.

It was uncanny. It always had been. She didn't understand it and never had, but it was as if there was something inside her that just knew when someone was being untruthful. Even as a small child Fergus hadn't been able to fool her. Once he'd even tried to tell her that her favorite nurse-maid had just gone ta visit family without saying goodbye. She'd known better. For one thing, Maggie had loved her and would never have left without a word, and for another, though still very young herself, she'd seen the signs of impending death on Maggie's face and knew the old woman's time had been drawing near.

Aila sighed as she set the brush down and laid upon the straw mattress of her small cot. Though she pulled the furs up around her shoulders, she shivered. It was summer, yet there was no true warmth to be found in this keep and especially not in this cold, lonely bed. To make matters worse, she well kenned it was mostly her fault. After all, Ian hadn't asked her to leave his bed. No, she'd done that all on her own. It'd been an act meant to punish him for not being truthful with her, but she was pretty sure she was the one feeling the sharpest sting.

Especially from the castle staff.

Though they followed her orders without question, she hadn't missed the looks of confusion and disgust gracing each of their faces. They did not like their laird being treated badly, and she couldn't blame them. She didn't like it either.

And she missed him.

God help her, but she missed him beyond reason.

She missed the smell of him, the weight of his arm thrown across her in sleep, the soft sound of his snore, the touch of his lips upon hers, and his lust-filled voice whispering words of want and desire close to her ear, and she missed him waking her from her slumber with those lips and hands.

She even missed being startled in the middle of the night when for some unknown reason he suddenly jumped up from their bed and rushed from their room as if the hounds of hell were nipping at his heels. But then, that was yet another thing he was untruthful about when asked.

What demons tormented her husband and why? For they certainly did.

God help her, but more than anything else, she sorely missed his magnificent cock filling her, stretching her, riding her, taking her to the very heavens and back down to earth again. Making her truly feel like a woman, making her feel bonny for the first time in her life.

God yes, she missed that cock, those smiling lips, those big strong arms, and even his lying tongue. God yes, especially that wonderfully, sinful tongue of his.

The private place between her legs hummed with need, throbbed with it even. It'd been so long, too long, since she'd last lain with her husband and felt the hot, heavy length and girth of him slip inside her, rock her gently at first, and then hard and fast, pumping, pounding, pleasuring. His lips kissing every inch of her body, his tongue flicking out sending spirals of decadent delight shooting right through every inch it touched, scorching her very soul.

Yes, Ian Mackay's cock and other parts were truly magnificent, just as magnificent as the mind of the stubborn, pig-headed man himself. Why couldn't he simply admit he'd been wrong and tell her the truth? Then life could get back to normal.

She rubbed her slightly rounded belly and smiled.

That wonderful cock of his had put their babe in there. And that was one thing his lies could never change.

Who would their bairn be?

Would their babe have hair as dark as the night like its da or red like hers? Would the lad be big and strong like his father? Or would the lass be slight like her mam? Would its eyes be stormy blue or forest green? Would its voice fill the castle with laughter? Would its reason for tears be few and far between?

She sighed once more and rolled over hugging the fur close to her body. He or she would be whoever they were, of that Aila had no doubt, and she'd love them with all her heart no matter what. She just hoped their babe was born without incident. She couldn't begin to count how many bairns she'd helped bring into this world, and thankfully most were kicking, screaming, and searching for their mam's teet only moments after sliding from the womb.

Old Margot's methods had proven tried and true, time after time after time. But who'd be there when it was her turn? For her child? There were no other healers for miles. Especially none who'd be willing to help deliver a Mackay bairn.

A single tear escaped, and Aila quickly swiped it away. She'd not give into her fear no matter how alone she felt. She was strong, she was smart, she was the lady of the keep, a healer, and the wife of the laird. She could do this. She would do this, even if she had to do it all by herself.

But by God, enough was enough, and she wasn't going to.

With her mind made up, Aila slipped from her cold, lonely bed and went in search of her husband.

****

For the tenth time in as many minutes, Ian yelled into the wind. "Fate? Tobias, you there? I need to talk to you. I really, really do."

Just like the nine previous attempts, his answer was nothing but silence.

He stood on a rocky outcropping by the sea with his hands cupped close to his mouth. The wind whipped his kilt about his legs and sea spray chilled his face. It might very well be what was considered summer in the highlands, but northern Scotland wasn't anything like the hot, muggy Ohio summers he'd been used to as a boy, let alone those hellishly hot Iraq and Afghanistan days. On the contrary, summer this far north of the equator was anything but hot. Though warm when the sun was directly upon him while working the fields or training the men, it never felt what he'd call hot, especially after the sun set.

He wrapped his plaid closer about himself and stared off into the distance. The sea was angry tonight, and it matched his mood. A storm was brewing. He could sense it. A storm completely separate from the one he'd been fighting with his wife.

As if he needed anymore problems right now.

But he could feel it, almost like an itch upon his skin or the rise of hair on the back of his neck, a premonition, so to speak. Just like the one he'd had that horrible day in Afghanistan when Danny and the others died. The fact he'd had to venture this far from the castle and the woman he loved just to attempt a conversation with Fate where no one else would see or hear only added to his frustration.

He shivered.

"Tobias, damn you," he shouted once more. "I need to ask you something important, so show yourself, you little prick. I don't have all night."

"I beg your pardon," Tobias Moiré, third generation event manipulator, harrumphed. "Little prick? I'll have you know the male side of the Moiré family of Fates is well known for being more than adequately endowed." Then he chuckled. "Just ask the seraphims, they'll tell you."

Ian stared at the specter before him.

He'd expected Fate to show up at some point, but it still surprised him to see the eerie, ghost-like figure suddenly rise from the middle of the waves and walk right up to him. Even stranger, Tobias's white robe wasn't in the least damp. On the contrary, he looked exactly as he always had—messy brown hair, wired-rimmed glasses, and all.

Fate shrugged his shoulders. "Well, spit it out then. I don't have all night, you know? Some of us have more responsibilities than seeing to the welfare of one small female, a half-built castle, and a few villagers. I was personally right in the middle of whipping up a hurricane, a small one mind you, but a hurricane all the same."

Ian shook his head. "Don't you ever take a day off from causing mischief? Wasn't it a blizzard you were working on last time? What about trying to do something good and nice for a change? You know, like perhaps an entire day when no one has to die or be hurt or go hungry or even have a reason to cry?"

Tobias tapped his foot and folded his arms across his chest. "Again, do I try and tell you how to do your job? You said you had a question. If so, what is it? I have other, much more important things to do than stand here chatting with the likes of you."

Fate began to shimmer, and Ian jumped toward him, as if he could somehow stop the man from disappearing. "No," he yelled. "I need to know if it's possible to use knowledge from the twenty-first century to make something for my wife without messing with the time line or whatever."

Tobias Moiré stopped shimmering. "Hmm, I suppose that would depend on what you plan on making. If you make her a nice pot of stew using your grandmother's recipe, I'd say that would probably be fine. You could even slightly improve the tools you use for farming as long as you don't go too far. No tractors or combines or such. And if you have something like those fancy new-fangled silk panties I've seen lately, or even a modern bra, in mind, then I'd have to say don't do it. Trust me, you don't want to deal with the headache of explaining how one of those contraptions works. Let alone having your people look at you like you're more of a freak than what they already think you to be."

He paused for a moment. "I mean really, Ian, what were you thinking? Trying to implement crop rotation in 1643 Scotland? Going on and on about how you wish to use fish guts for fertilizer? And specifically telling them it's because they need to increase the nitrogen levels in the soil? As if 1643 farmers know what nitrogen is?

"And then you put the topping on the cake by making friends with their enemy the Sutherlands, repairing their sails and visiting their castle? "Have you lost your mind?"

Ian took a deep breath but didn't say anything. He might as well let Fate run his course, because there certainly was no getting a word in edgewise until Tobias was finished ranting.

"And why are you so bent on making something from your time for your wife anyway," Fate asked. "Piss her off, did you? She kicked you out of your bed?"

Ian glanced down at his feet. "She doesn't believe that Ian Mackay didn't die that night, and she's pissed because she thinks I'm lying to her." He looked back up and squarely met Tobias's eyes. "So since I can't tell her the truth, I thought I'd make her something. Girls like gifts, right?"

Fate shook his head. "Why not just tell her the truth?"

Ian just stared at him. "Probably because there's no way in hell she's ever going to believe what really did happen. I can't blurt out I'm from the fucking future and living in some dead guy's body."

"Why not," Tobias asked.

Ian sighed. "Because it's fucking 1643 and no one in their right mind would believe I, or anyone else, traveled back through time."

Fate shrugged again. "Then make her a stupid gift. It probably won't work, and you'll still have to tell her the truth eventually, but hey, your life, your wife." He chuckled. "So what exactly are you thinking about constructing?"

Heat flooded his cheeks. Ian didn't know why he thought Tobias Moiré would make fun of him for his idea, but he was pretty sure he would. He'd never really been the frivolous type. On the contrary, if anything, he'd always been way too practical for his own good.

He took a deep breath as heat creeped up his neck and filled his cheeks. "Aila has this thing about her...her teeth. She's constantly picking at them with a stupid stick. Says people live longer if they do. So I thought perhaps I'd make her a...a toothbrush." He took another deep breath. "I can whittle the shape from a small piece of wood, bore a few holes in it, and use pig hair for the bristles."

"Who says chivalry is dead?" Fate smirked a mere second before beginning to shimmer once more. "You, Ian Mackay, are a true romantic. That's for certain. But I have no more time for your fumbling love life. Buck up and do whatever it is you need to do to make the lass like you again, even if that means telling her the truth. Trust me when I say, with time all things work out, eventually."

Tobias was almost completely gone when Ian remembered there was one more thing he'd really needed to talk over with Fate. "Wait! Something else is wrong, too. I can't explain it, but I just have the feeling that something bad is going to happen. It's a feeling I've had before. Right before Danny and the others died. It's beginning to creep me out."

Tobias Moiré came back into focus. "Of course, something bad is going to happen. On any given day of any given year, there is always something bad about to happen. That's called life. The question is, have you prepared yourself and your men for whatever it may be? Because that's really all you can do. You changed history when you entered Ian Mackay's body, and changing history has its own price to pay. Let's just hope the cost isn't too steep this time around."

Again, Fate began to shimmer.

"Wait," Ian yelled. "I forgot to tell you she's pregnant. Aila, that is. It looks like I'm going to be a father. Or at least Ian Mackay is going to be a father. What am I supposed to do about that? I don't know the first thing about being anybody's dad, or even if I'll be in this time period long enough to see a child raised. "And speaking of how long I'm going to be here, when do I get the chance to redo what happened that day in Afghanistan?"

The chuckle he heard was no more than the whisper of the wind as Tobias Moiré disappeared completely out of sight, but Ian understood every word.

"You're free to go back when you like. After all, you've done what you promised to do. But since you're soon to become a father, I seriously doubt you're ready to do that yet. Bravo and congratulations on your upcoming offspring, though, and be sure to let me know when you are truly ready to return to that fateful day. There is no hurry, though. It's not as if any of them have even been born yet."

****

"Are ye talking ta yerself again then, laird?"

Ian whipped around, knowing exactly what little face awaited him, and sighed. "Daniel, how many times must I tell you we have guards to keep watch? You can sleep at night like all the other children."

The lad scrunched up his face. "I thank ye for that, laird. Really I do. But I'll nae be breaking me promise ta the old laird. I'll be keeping me own watch. Especially since ye are still titched in the head and wander about. Does her ladyship ken ye come out here and talk ta yerself most every night?"

He wanted to be angry. He wanted to yell at the kid that it wasn't any of his business what his laird did, but he didn't have the heart. He probably did look like a lunatic. Hell, there'd been times, since arriving in 1643 Scotland, that he had very much doubted his sanity.

But Ian settled for shrugging and smiling at the child instead. "No, Daniel, her ladyship does not know I am titched in the head and wander about at night, and you'd better not be telling her or anyone else, either. Sometimes I just need time alone to think things through out loud and to clear my mind. It's a heavy responsibility being laird."

Daniel smiled back, and his crooked little grin made Ian's heart ache for a moment as it reminded him of his long-lost friend and the responsibility awaiting him when he did finally leave this time.

Chapter Fourteen

This entire situation had grown far beyond ridiculous.

Aila paced the floor of Ian's room and got angrier with each step she took.

The stubborn man was avoiding her. He'd risen long before the sun this verra morning, and she well kenned it. She'd been watching for him. And now he was not in his bed and it was well into the night.

He hadn't even spoken more than a handful of words to her in days, and then only if she happened to catch a glimpse of him on his way back out to wherever it was or whomever it was he was spending his time with these days. For one thing was certain, he wasn't spending it anywhere near her.

It had to be another woman. She sighed, and her eyes burned with unshed tears. No other explanation made any sense. And she wasn't sure who she was angrier with, him or herself. She been hard to live with lately, and she'd done her best to make him as miserable as she possibly could because he hadn't told her the truth.

But had she gone too far this time?

Hadn't Fergus warned her time and again about her stubbornness, her willfulness? And how some day it would be her downfall?

Had she driven her husband straight into the arms

of another woman? And if she had, what could she do about it now?

So what if Ian hadn't been entirely truthful about the night she thought he'd died? Perhaps he himself didn't understand or remember everything that happened. After all, the last time she'd seen him before walking into that room, he'd been falling-down drunk, and it was common knowledge that a man well into his cups rarely remembered his actions come the next morn.

And if Ian Mackay was visiting another lass's bed right this very moment, could she even blame him? After all, she hadn't given him much choice, had she? She'd been the one to leave the warmth and comfort of his arms and had even forbidden him to so much as seek her out until he was ready to tell her the truth.

But men rule this world, not women, and well she kenned it. After all, she'd spent her entire life before Ian at the beck and call of her brother.

So what was she to do now?

It's not as if she could go door-to-door searching. Even if it hadn't been well after dark, her pride wouldn't allow it. Not that the entire staff of the castle wasn't already aware their laird and his lady wife weren't sharing the same bed. Oh no, every single one of them kenned it, because there was no keeping a secret in a keep. You couldn't even make a trip to the garderobe for a healthy shit without half the clan taking notice and commenting on it.

No, she couldn't go searching for him in the middle of the night, but there was nothing stopping her from climbing into his bed and waiting for him to get back. And return soon, he'd better. For God help Ian Mackay if she caught so much as a whiff of another woman's scent upon his skin when he did walk back through that door. Husband or no, she'd make him dearly regret it, and for a verra long time.

Men may very well rule the world, but a woman is not powerless. And if Ian Mackay was cheating on her, she knew of more than a few herbs that'd make sure that magnificent cock of his never again rose to the task of diddling someone else's cunny.

But then another thought struck her. If a man was well satisfied in his bed, he had no reason to stray. And one thing was certain, she hadn't been satisfying anyone or anything of late except for her own bitterness. Perhaps it was time to put that childish anger behind her.

So what if he never told her the truth about what happened the night she thought him dead? Could she live with not knowing?

Aye, she could.

But what she couldn't fathom was a life without him in it, especially now that she knew he was no *sidhe* but a real live, warm flesh and blood man.

Since they'd been at Borve castle, her life had changed so much and all because of Ian. She was a lady of the keep now, but only because she was his wife. And she was accepted by the Mackays because of him. She was not only allowed to practice her healing but was encouraged to. And when he touched her, it was with tenderness and passion, and even when she was angry at him, he was still kind to her. His smile brightened her day, and the sound of his voice made her heart soar. And the sight of him turned her insides to butter.

Aila gasped as a realization hit her. She really was completely in love with her husband. God help her, but she was.

When had that happened? She'd tried so hard to prevent it.

And she didn't just love him, but even worse, she was kilt over kittle deeply in love with the man. The knowledge caught her by surprise.

So then, what should she do now?

It was with a sly smile she yanked her shift up over her head and tossed it to the floor. Naked as the day she was born, Aila Mackay climbed into Ian's bed to wait. Oh aye, it was certainly a bonny cock the man had betwixt his legs, and it was hers and no one else's. The rest of the man, too.

That's exactly what she was still thinking when the door opened a moment later.

"Come ta bed, husband. I'm chilled," she whispered across the expanse of the room.

That seemed to be all the incentive he needed. He dropped his kilt to the floor without a word, stepped out of his boots, and quickly joined her.

His arms were cool from being outside in the night air, but his hands were wonderfully hot upon her skin, and his warm breath sent shivers of anticipation skittering along her spine as he whispered back, "I've missed you, wife."

****

Her skin was like fresh, warm cream beneath his fingertips, all smooth and silky and soft. She smelled of heather and honey and happiness and home. God, how he'd missed her. He hadn't even realized how much until he'd walked through the door only moments before and found her in his bed.

Ian closed his eyes and inhaled her essence deep within himself. When had this itty-bitty fireball of a woman become so important to his very existence? When she smiled, he smiled, and when Aila wasn't happy, then neither was he.

She squirmed beneath him and sighed. "Ian, ye can take all the time ye want the next go round, but right now, I need ta feel ye inside me."

He smiled against the soft, supple skin of her neck as he parted her thighs and quickly entered her. Warmth. That's what being inside Aila Mackay was. Slick, moist, slipping and sliding, pumping and plundering, straight from heaven warmth encompassed his cock and made its way to the very center of his soul. A warmth that filled him from the roots of his hair to the tips of his toes.

She lifted up toward him, sliding him in even deeper while playfully nipping at the tender skin of his neck. His mind blurred, and he lost what little self-control he still possessed.

Grabbing her by the hips, he slammed his cock home over and over. And it wasn't until her sweet pussy clenched his length in satisfaction that his own orgasm exploded. He couldn't have wiped the smile off his face if his life had depended upon it. All he could think was, if there truly was a heaven somewhere, then it must start and end in this woman's arms.

But a heartbeat later, he remembered his wife was with child and he'd been anything but gentle.

"Oh, my God, Aila. I didn't hurt you or the babe, did I?" He gasped. "Please tell me I didn't."

She had the audacity to giggle and then wiggle

162

against him. "Nae, Ian, ye did nae hurt me or our bairn. We both are fine as frog's hair."

He rolled over and snuggled her firmly against his side with her head resting just above his heart. "I'll never do anything intentionally to hurt you, lass. I swear I won't."

She kissed his nipple and then playfully nipped it. "I ken ye'd nae ever strike me, Ian. Ye are nae that kind of man." She sighed and snuggled in closer. "And I am verra tired of being angry at ye for lying ta me. That did hurt me, deeply, but I want ta live in peace with ye, husband. So if ye do nae ever wish ta tell me the truth, then so be it. I'll nae ask again."

It was Ian's turn to sigh. He knew how important the truth between two people could be, especially a man and a woman. And how being untruthful with one's mate, even in small things, could completely destroy a relationship.

In the marines, there were things that couldn't be shared, not even with a spouse. Since he'd been a staff sergeant, with men beneath him, he'd seen his share of Dear John letters after the wives grew tired of never knowing what their husbands were up to or where they were. During his three deployments, he'd talked more solders back from the abyss of utter despair than he'd like to think about.

He didn't want to push Aila that far, or away, but then he didn't want to tell her the truth either. Because what really had happened was crazier than her first thought of him being some kind of fucking fairy.

Then again, how could he ever expect her to trust him if he was never honest with her? It was a wedge between them, and a wedge that would continue to grow and widen until the expanse became impossible to cross.

What difference would it make if he did tell her the truth? It wasn't as if he was going to be in this time period for much longer anyway. He'd stay until the crops were harvested, the fishing was done for the year, and the babe was born, and then he'd go back and redo that last day in Afghanistan. He'd save his best friend and the others.

Aila and the Mackays would be able to take care of themselves by then. They'd no longer need him.

In the meantime, there'd finally be peace between him and his wife. Even if she did think him completely crazy after she heard what he had to say. Crazy was better than being a liar. Wasn't it?

With his mind made up, Ian lifted Aila into his arms so that they were eye to eye. "You're right. You should know the truth. But it's a truth that must remain between the two of us. If anyone else was to find out, it could end very badly."

She didn't say a word but simply nodded her head.

He took a deep breath, trying to decide just how to start. Then he took another and another.

She swatted at him playfully and smiled. "Ye have ta actually begin yer story before ye can ever get ta the end of it, ye ken?"

He took one more deep breath and closed his eyes. He didn't want to see the same look of disbelief and hurt on her face as he'd seen the last time they tried to have this conversation. "What I'm about to tell you is going to sound crazy and impossible, but I swear on everything I hold dear that it's the truth, the whole truth, and nothing but the truth."

He shook his head slightly as he finally came to terms with what he was about to do. Opening his eyes, he gazed at his wife, pleading silently for her to believe him.

"I'm from the future, Aila," he spat out. "Almost four hundred years from now to be exact. But I'm not from this body you now see me in. You were right. The original Ian Mackay was dead that night you found him. He was one of my ancestors, you see, and we shared the same name and linage. When I died in an accident—in the future—Fate himself sent me back into the past and into this Ian Mackay's body to correct a mistake that should never have happened in the first place."

"What should nae have happened, Ian?" she asked.

He gulped. "Your death, Aila."

Her eyes widened, and he held her even tighter. "In the original time, one of Mackay's men saw you fleeing Ian's room that night and you were put to death for the Mackay's murder the very next day. Your brother had the deed done, but it wasn't as if he had a choice. It was by direct order of the king."

She shuddered in his arms, and he held her closer. "But you don't have to worry about that now, you see. We've changed history. Ian Mackay didn't really die this time, and neither did you. And now we are here at Borve castle together, and you're the lady of the keep, and with child, our child. You have your whole life ahead of you. We both do."

****

Aila didn't know how it could be so, but what Ian had just told her was the truth. She'd bet her very life on it. From what he'd said, it seemed her very life had been in question. She shuddered again, and her husband's arms wrapped her in even closer than before.

Her husband, her Ian Mackay, not the drunkard who'd come calling at her brother's castle after all. That explained so much.

That's why this Ian Mackay didn't flirt or ogle everything in a shirt. That's why this Ian Mackay didn't talk with his hands flapping like a goose or drink like a fish. And that's why this Ian Mackay was nothing like any of the other highlanders she'd ever met.

This Ian had allowed her to treat their people's needs and never once worried about any risk to his own health. He'd talked to her as if they were friends instead of her just being his wife. He worked right alongside the villagers and the fisherman doing whatever needed to be done, instead of giving orders from his seat at the high table for other men to do. He was kind to children, especially young Daniel, and always took the time to answer the lad's questions. And he'd touched her with such tenderness every time they made love, he'd brought her herbs of all things, he'd laughed when she laughed, and he'd held her when she'd cried.

All the while, she'd been a fool not to see the truth in him.

That was one mistake she intended nae to make again.

She had questions for him, so many questions she didn't know where to begin. But they weren't what she wanted to ask of him right now. This moment was too fragile, too new, and too precious to waste on mere questions. These next few moments and how she reacted to what he'd had to say were extremely important. For Ian, her Ian, was staring at her with what looked to be fear in his eyes. It was obvious he had no idea what she was going to say.

It was her turn to take a deep breath. "Put ye wonderful cock inside me, Ian. Please, me husband, me fae man from the future," she whispered. "I have a powerful need ta feel ye deep within me once again." Then she giggled. "Especially since ye've traveled such a long way and time just ta be here with me, and ye saved me life ta boot." She wiggled against his warm, semi-soft groin, and he groaned.

For a moment, his eyes clouded over. "You still don't believe me, do you? I swear I'm not lying to you, Aila. I really am from almost four hundred years in the future."

She smiled and wiggled once more before draping a leg about him. "Oh, I believe ye, Ian. Honestly, I do. It just seems ta me that time must really be verra precious indeed if ye came all this way just ta save me. And I aim ta nae waste another moment of it."

She wrapped her arms about his neck and captured his mouth in a kiss she hoped conveyed her belief in him more than any words could.

And suddenly, Ian's cock wasn't the least bit soft anymore.

Chapter Fifteen

September 1643
Borve Castle

The first rays of morning sun were just beginning to find their way into the chamber as Aila watched her husband sleep. Lord help her, but he was bonny to look upon. She gloried in the fact that she was at least partially responsible for the fact Ian hadn't fled their bed to god knew where in the middle of the night, like he had so many times before, but had slept peacefully by her side the entire night through.

She chuckled to herself. Had it been three or four times they'd made love throughout the night? Touched, caressed, kissed, whispered, and held onto each other as if their very lives depended upon it. As if they'd both been desperate to make up for the time they'd lost.

Time. She sighed. What a strange thing time was. The thought that her husband, her Ian Mackay, had traveled back through time almost four hundred years, just to save her, was even harder to comprehend.

She had so many questions to ask him, so many thoughts running through her mind, but no idea where to begin.

For one thing, Ian had said that in the original time she had died at the hands of her brother and at the king's insistence because they thought her responsible for Ian's death. How exactly had she died? Had Fergus regretted doing what he'd been ordered to do to her? Had she been buried in the family plot as was her due, or were her disgraced ashes simply tossed to the wind and forgotten?

Aila shuddered, the morbid thoughts sending chills skittering along her spine.

To rid herself of them, she concentrated instead on the sight of her husband still sleeping so peacefully. What demons drove him from their bed on so many nights? For something surely did. Something he was reluctant to speak of. Something that troubled him deeply.

He'd told her that his other life had ended in an accident. What had happened? Had he been a young man cut down in his prime, or had he lived a long full life before that fateful day? Who was he really, his likes and dislikes? Did he leave behind a wife and bairns he'd dearly loved?

She hoped not.

Did he regret his life with her now?

And what of the world he'd came from?

Were there still wars in his time, or had men finally learned to live in peace with one another? Were there kings and queens ruling the lands, lairds to bow down to, and poor to be cared for? Or were all now equal and happy and free? Were lands still owned by the few and worked by the many? Was there plenty to eat? Was sickness a thing of the past? And if so, what miracle herbs had been found to bring about such a glorious thing? Were sons still valued above daughters? And were women still naught but chattel in their husband's eyes?

She hoped not.

She thought perhaps nae.

For this Ian, her Ian, had certainly never treated her thusly.

She snuggled in closer around him, content to listen to the sound of his breathing and the beat of his heart. To feel his warmth, to touch his skin, to simply be in his presence. Wherever or whenever this magical Ian Mackay had come from, he was hers now and forever and she was reluctant to let him go.

Suddenly, there was a flutter deep in the pit of her belly, like the gentle sweep of angel wings, and she couldn't contain her smile. Her bairn, their bairn, was also letting his presence be known this fine morning.

A moment later, her smiled died. Fergus would find out about the babe soon, of that she had no doubt. She'd bet her life the man had planted at least one of his spies within spitting distance of Borve castle. A spy who, no doubt, made regular trips back to Skelbo.

Fergus would come before the first snow of winter fell, forcing him to remain close to home. When he arrived at Borve, he'd do exactly what he swore he'd do. He'd kill her and the bairn.

Fergus Gordon did not make idle threats. He never had.

Guilt filled her. The fact a threat had been made in the first place was a bit of information she'd kept from Ian. She'd wanted to keep peace between the Gordons and the Mackays. And frankly, she hadn't thought to say anything to him before now because she'd been convinced he was a *sidhe* and could not father a child.

But she'd been wrong, and now a bairn was well on its way, a half Gordon, half Mackay babe. A child her brother swore would nae ever draw a breath.

She shuddered.

Ian had a right to know, a responsibility even. It was his bairn, too. And like it or nae, it was time to be as honest with her husband as he'd been with her.

****

Ian watched Aila come up over the rise and wondered what was bothering his pretty little wife now? Because if the fact she was furiously chewing at her bottom lip was any indication, something was definitely weighing heavy on Aila Mackay's mind, and he just hoped it wasn't him this time.

He'd told her the truth of how he'd gotten here, or at least as much truth as he thought she could take and understand. He had no idea what questions she might have left or how to even begin to answer them. To make matters worse, he really didn't have time for it today. There were fields to be inspected and the quality of their output to be apprised.

But time to deal with it or not was irrelevant, because she certainly wasn't turning around, and the closer she came, the faster she chewed that lip.

"How did ye say ye died, again?" Aila asked once she was within speaking distance.

For a moment, Ian simply stared at her. She'd walked all the way from the castle to the most northern field on Borve property just to ask him that?

At first, he was angry. Really? Couldn't this have waited until later tonight? Couldn't she see he was busy?

Then the sheen of tears glistening in her moss-green eyes stopped him in his tracks. She was young, she was obviously frightened by all he'd told her, and not only was she pregnant and very vulnerable, but she was his wife and deserved the best he could give her.

"It was a truck accident," he answered.

She chewed that poor lip once more. "And is a truck a kind of weapon by chance? Like a claymore, perhaps, or even a plain sword or arrow?"

Ian shook his head. "No, a truck is a vehicle, kind of like a wagon, but it doesn't use horses to pull it along. It has what's called an engine, which makes it go very fast. I simply lost control of it, and it cost me my life."

"Oh," she said, then began wringing her hands. "Ye do ken how ta use weapons, though, do ye nae? I mean, most men can. Ian Mackay—I mean the other Ian Mackay—was well-regarded when it came ta the use of a claymore."

Ian nodded, not sure how to answer her question. Was it fear *of* him or *for* him that drove her questions? Had she finally come to the realization that he really wasn't the Ian Mackay she'd known?

In the end, he settled for the truth. "Yes, Aila, I know quite a bit about weapons. In my other life, I was a soldier and fought in wars."

She stared back at him for a moment and then visibly relaxed. "Good, because I do nae want me brither ta kill ye outright."

It was Ian's turn to stare. "What are you talking about? Perhaps we'd better start this conversation over, because frankly, I'm lost."

With a sob, she ran straight into his arms. "I should've told ye sooner. I ken I should've. I just did nae think it mattered, 'cause ye were a *sidhe* then. Or at least I thought ye were a *sidhe*. But now ye are nae, and now I am with child, and now Fergus will be coming ta kill us all."

He wrapped his arms around her tighter and kissed the top of her head. "Shhhhh. "I won't let anyone ever hurt you or our child. I promise. Not even your brother. Especially not your brother."

She sniffed. "But what if ye are nae here? What if ye are snatched back up and placed into someone else's body in some other time? How do ye ken that won't happen again?"

He really didn't have any idea how to answer that question and guilt filled him. Hadn't he himself been thinking about when he would leave? When he would go back and try to save Danny and his men? But he had to, in some way, comfort his wife.

"There's no need to worry. I'm not going anywhere, Aila. I'm staying right here by your side where I belong."

And he hoped with all his heart and soul that he meant it.

****

Fergus Gordon needed to die.

And not just fall over dead but die the slowest most painful death humanly possible.

How could any man, especially a woman's own flesh-and-blood brother, threaten to kill an innocent little baby and its mother just because its father was a Mackay?

Ian stood with his back to Borve castle, watching the waves hit the beach, hoping the solitude would do what nothing else had been able to accomplish for him today. He needed to calm down. He needed to think. He needed to plan, and he couldn't do any of those things while wanting to ride straight to Skelbo castle and slit

Fergus Gordon's throat.

His fingers itched with the need to do just that.

Aila had trembled when she told him what her brother had said. Tears had filled her lovely green eyes and overflowed upon her small, soft pink cheeks. She'd wept in his arms, and she'd begged him not to do anything rash. Not to go running off after her brother. That without proof of intent, the king would side with Fergus, and rightly so.

But he couldn't very well just sit here and wait for the man to harm his wife and child either. And, by God, they were his. Even if he was in another man's body and had used that man's cock to impregnate said wife in the first place.

That Ian Mackay had been a total idiot. He'd thrown his life away without a second thought, and Ian himself had merely been lucky enough to be in the right place and time to take up where the drunken sod left off.

Ian shook his head. When had driving too fast, flipping his truck, and killing himself constituted right place right time? But strangely it had. And now that he really was here, in 1643 Scotland of all places, and Aila Mackay's husband to boot, hell would freeze over before he'd allow anyone to harm her or their kid.

But he had to be smart about it.

She was right. He couldn't go off half-cocked. Especially since they were so outnumbered.

Fergus had the Gordons and a good part of the Sutherlands at his disposal. An army of great big well-trained, claymore-swinging, hand-to-hand fighting highlanders while all Ian had to depend upon was a bunch of farmers and fisherman.

But Ian knew very well that numbers and size didn't always win the day. Heart and strategy would triumph over arrogance and hatred every time given that the strategy was the right one. If his multiple tours of duty in Iraq and Afghanistan while with the Marine Corp had taught him anything, it had been strategy.

There's always a way to overcome, a way to win the day. He just needed to be vigilant, and he needed to be smart. What were his enemy's weaknesses, and how could he exploit them to his advantage? Even more importantly, what were their strengths and how could he best undermine them at every turn?

Though a mentally wounded one, he was still a soldier at heart. Once a marine, always a marine the saying went. Semper Fi! He could do this. He had no choice. Even Fate had told him to be a soldier and protect his people. He could protect them. He *would* protect them. He just needed a plan.

The very beginning of an idea began to form. Although it was true he hadn't paid much attention in history class, earth science and chemistry had been a whole different story. He'd loved both subjects. Especially the parts where he got to do projects and mix stuff together with other stuff to get a reaction.

Ian chuckled as the memory of his father's face when told his son had almost blown up the science lab came to mind. The poor man had turned a scary shade of gray and then an almost purple before grabbing up Ian and marching him to the car. He hadn't said a single word all the way home, but the moment the car had stopped, he'd had one and only one word to say. *Woodshed.*

And that one word had been more than enough.

That whooping with a willow tree switch had been one he'd never forgotten. His father hadn't been one to discipline lightly, it took quite a bit of provocation to push the man that far. But Ian knew he'd literally blasted past his father's limit when he'd used his old man's own recipe for black powder in an attempt to impress a girl of all things. And even though Danny had tried his best to dissuade him from his folly, Amy Lynn Havisham, with her bouncy, blonde curls and pouty, pink lips had certainly been worth the whooping.

But more importantly, he'd bet his left nut that gunpowder hadn't been used very often in 1643 Scotland and would catch Fergus Gordon off guard. From what he'd seen of this time period, most highlanders just used big assed swords and sharp little daggers.

Wouldn't dear ole Fergus be just a wee bit surprised if Ian blew his fucking ass up?

The thought brought the first smile of the day to his face.

Now all he needed to do was talk with his men and find himself some sulfur and charcoal. The potassium nitrate, or salt peter, he was going to have to make himself, and he knew just how to go about that, too.

****

"Ye want us ta what?"

Ian almost felt sorry for Daniel...almost. But the look on the lad's face when given the order he'd just been given, had been beyond priceless. If he hadn't really thought his laird titched in the head before today, he certainly did now.

"I said, now that you and the other lads have filled the barrels with horse dung, pig shit, and dirt as I asked you to do, I want all of you to piss in them. Fill 'em up good. The more piss the better. Every time you get the urge, all day long today, come and relive yourselves in these barrels.

"I'll even get ya started."

He took a stance directly over one of the four barrels, lifted the hem of his kilt, and let loose with a steamy, steady yellow stream.

Daniel fidgeted on one leg. "That's what I thought ye said, laird." Then he gestured toward the other boys. "Ye heard what his lairdship said." Lifting his own kilt, Daniel proceeded to do as he'd been told, but not quietly. "So, why are we pissing on the shit? I mean, ye must have a good reason, don't ye? Other than being a little titched, that is."

Ian chuckled. He'd asked his own father that very same question once after spending the better part of a day filling barrels with equal parts soil and overly ripe horse manure.

"Manure is premium shit, boy," his father had answered. "We're making potassium nitrate for the black powder outta it. You don't think those stumps blow themselves outta the ground, now do ya?"

His dad could've used cold packs or bottled stump remover as salt peter, but he'd been a stickler for following the original recipe to a tee, and if he could see Ian right now, tainting the precious horse manure with pig shit, he'd probably take him back out to the woodshed for another round with the willow tree switch. But there had been no other choice. Sadly, they owned more pigs than they did horses, so turning pig shit into potassium nitrate/salt peter was just going to have to work.

But he didn't say any of that to Daniel. Instead, he simply replied, "We're making a surprise for Aila's brother and the Sutherlands, for when and if they decide to come calling."

Daniel's face lit up like a candle. "We gonna throw wet shit at um, then? I would nae mind tossing shit balls at a Sutherland or two. If anyone deserves ta be covered in shit, it'd be a Sutherland. Yep, shitty Sutherlands, the whole lot of um."

For a moment, Ian felt a stab of guilt for not correcting Daniel's oblivious pleasure in using the word shit, over and over. If the young lad had grown up in Ian's mother's house, his mouth would've been washed out with soap ten times over by now, and his backside would be stinging. But this wasn't bible-belt, farming community, Amish country, Johnsville, Ohio. This was 1643 Scotland, and if shit was the worst thing young Daniel said today, they'd all be lucky.

"No, we aren't going to throw it at them," Ian said, though the thought did have some merit. "We're going to dry it. Then we're going to mix it with charcoal and sulfur and hopefully blow their asses up. So only piss in it today. We need it to dry out into a powder before too long."

Daniel shook his head and frowned. "Ye truly are titched in the head, laird. Shit is just shit, and ya can nae blow up shit no matter what ye mix it with. Everybody knows that. But I'll piss on it all day long if it makes ye happy. And so will the other lads. Ye just wait and see if we don't."

Young Daniel hadn't been the only one to think their laird a little titched in the head today either. The look on Brody's face when he informed the grisly old fisherman that he was confiscating every stick of wood not yet attached to a boat had been a sight.

Though fields of heather were abundant, trees were scarce this far north. Wood was hard to come by on a good day and today wasn't a very good day. That was why peat had been used here for heat for centuries. But peat couldn't be burned down into charcoal like wood could. Charcoal was an essential ingredient in the making of black powder, and if they were going to survive an attack by the Gordons and the Sutherlands, they were going to need all the black powder they could make.

Materials to repair boats would just have to wait for another day.

But the sulfur was going to be the hardest mineral to obtain. Not that he didn't know exactly where to find it. All the sulfur he could ever want or need could be found to the west in Tongue.

At first, he hadn't remembered where that little tid-bit of information had come from, and then suddenly he did. It was a memory from the original Ian Mackay. Castle Varrich, the seat of the Mackays and the home of William Mackay, the man who hated him and had wanted him dead, sat right dab in the middle of stinky Tongue.

Great. Just fucking great.

Sulfur springs were only abundant in and around Tongue, Scotland, which was just a few days ride north-west of Borve castle. And it wasn't bad enough that Tongue was where William Mackay would be, but right between here and there were the lands of the Sutherland clan who'd killed the old Mackay, and of course, Fergus Gordon and his bunch. Which meant, in order to get the much-needed sulfur, Ian was going to have to come within spitting distance of not only the Sutherlands and William Mackay, but also Aila's crazy brother. And he was going to have to do it without any of the Mackays, Gordons, or Sutherlands, scattered about everywhere, being any the wiser.

At least *most* of the other Sutherlands, that was.

But he had a plan.

He meant to hide in plain sight.

It was time to call in that favor from Stephen Sutherland. That was, just as soon as he found his wife and explained to her what he had in mind. Then he'd find old Brody and make sure the crotchety old fisherman would, not only still speak to him, but also keep a close eye on Aila while he was away.

Chapter Sixteen

Late September 1643
Borve Castle

Aila crossed to the window, stared down at the bailey below, and sighed.

He wasn't there. Just as he hadn't been there for days now. It wasn't as if she'd really expected to see him. It was simply habit to look. For Ian was long gone from Borve lands and well on his way to Tongue with Stephen Sutherland, if not actually already there by now.

A part of her had wanted to go with him.

She'd longed to visit Stephen's wife Maggie again and to see how the babe she'd delivered was fairing. Good, she hoped. But it wasn't uncommon for peril, disease, and god-knew-what to snatch away a life before it even had a chance to begin. Even in this age of increased knowledge.

In the end, that was the real reason she decided to stay put where she was.

Not that Ian would've ever agreed for her to go with him in the first place, but because she couldn't allow herself to risk the child she carried to whatever dangers lay ahead for her husband.

He was taking a huge chance traveling so close to enemy Sutherland, Gordon and the Laird Mackay lands in order to get sulfur for his concoction. That's why she'd told him to go while she still slept. Had insisted upon it even. She couldn't bear to watch him leave knowing, that if spotted by her brother, his men, the other Sutherlands, or even his own laird, William Mackay, she'd probably never lay eyes on him again.

She'd even lied to him and told him she'd be perfectly fine with the old fisherman Brody keeping an eye out for her and the bairn. When in reality, she'd never be fine again without Ian by her side.

She shook her head. All this useless fidgeting and worry certainly wasn't making the heaviness in her heart any lighter or the time without him go by any faster.

It wasn't as if she'd had any real choice in the matter of him leaving on this dangerous mission in the first place. Ian had been right. If they were to have any kind of advantage over Fergus and the Sutherlands, then he did need to follow through with his plan and gather the ingredients for the burning powder he'd spoke of. And though she still had no real idea what mixing sulfur, salt peter, and charcoal together did exactly, she trusted that a man from so far into the future did.

Black powder, he'd called it. It sounded very English to her, and Aila wrinkled her nose.

He'd said that properly placed, the powder would burn and ward off the fiercest of attacks, and she dearly hoped he was right. For Fergus Gordon was a fierce warrior indeed. He'd never been bested in a battle, and just the speaking of his name had weans all over the lands scampering to hide behind their mams' skirt tails in fear, and for good reason.

It would take much more than a little smoke, fire,

and noise to scare off her brother, let alone The Sutherland or his men. But since peace between the two clans had been the dictate of the king himself, perhaps the Sutherlands wouldn't be so quick to defy King Charles this time and aid Fergus Gordon in his current endeavor.

But then again, that particular band of Sutherlands didn't take kindly to being told what to do, even by their king. So would they then ride beside Fergus and spite their liege? Only time would tell.

And even if the Sutherlands didn't come along, Fergus Gordon was just arrogant enough to ride right up to the walls of Borve and demand entrance along with his sister's head for daring to break her promise to him.

The question was, would old Brody and the rest of the villagers be able to keep Fergus at bay if he arrived before Ian and his burning powder got back? Even if they could, would it be fair to ask fisherman and farmers to risk their lives for her? Even though they all treated her with kindness and respect, she'd still been born a Gordon and their sworn enemy.

But she couldn't worry about it anymore, not right now anyway. There was a castle to run, chores to see to, meals to plan, and the sick to tend. Worry would simply have to wait until later. Perhaps tonight, after the castle was dark and all were snuggled in their beds sleeping peacefully.

All but her anyway.

For since Ian left, there'd been little sleep to be had. She wasn't even sure if it was because she missed her husband dearly or because old Brody insisted on sleeping right outside her chamber door each night, and the man snored so loudly she was surprised he hadn't awakened the dead.

And it wasn't just his snoring that was so irritating either. He treated her like a wean, following her around from room to room as if any moment she'd fall and scrape a knee or bump her head. It was maddening.

Of all the highlanders at Borve castle to choose from, why had her husband chosen the cantankerous, grizzled old fisherman, with foul breath and piss-poor manners to watch over her?

She was a woman full grown. She didn't need anyone to scrutinize her every move, and she certainly didn't need the likes of Brody Mackay for anything.

****

Long before he caught his first glimpse of Tongue's sulfur pools, Ian smelled them.

The acidy fragrance brought with it an unexpected wave of homesickness. With the planting of the fields, repairing the castle walls, seeing to the fisherman, and a pregnant wife, it'd been quite a while since he'd thought about his life before waking in 1643 Scotland.

Like how many lazy Sunday afternoons had he spent as a youth making black powder with his dad while his mom was busy in the kitchen cooking them up her special recipe, fried chicken, cornbread, soup beans, and collard greens?

His mouth watered.

And how many 45 caliber bullets for his old man's muzzleloader had he heated the lead for and slowly poured into molds? How many times had he melted them back down and redone the entire batch when they hadn't been quite up to his father's high standards?

More than he could count on both hands. That was

for sure.

But then the whole bullet making process and his perfectionist father had taught him patience, to never settle for doing anything half-ass, and to take pride in a job well done. It was a lesson that had served him well over the years.

The thought brought a smile to his face. Making the black powder and those stupid bullets had been the one true passion both he and his dad had shared.

Though Ian might very well have despised farming, he'd always loved hunting and shooting, especially with the antique weapon his father had inherited from his father, and his father from his, and so forth and so forth. It would've been his one day, to pass down to his son, if he'd lived long enough to receive it.

He wondered for a moment who would end up with the old muzzle loader. Both of his parents had been only children just as he had, so there were no immediate close relatives. His old man would probably just hand it over to a museum or something.

The thought brought with it a wave of sadness. He hadn't liked the gun just because it'd been a family heirloom. He'd loved it because of who it belonged to and because hunting with it was more of a challenge and somehow seemed fairer in the long run.

His father had once told him, "Even a blind man can hit the side of a barn from eighty yards given the right scope, calm winds, and shiny new bullets. But with the muzzleloader, son, it takes skill, not luck."

Not that there had been an abundance of wild game to be hunted in itty-bitty Johnsville, Ohio. Just the occasional rabbit, squirrel, random small deer, turkey, pheasant, or if desperate, those nasty-ass, fucking irritating crows that seemed to be everywhere all the time. But with the old muzzleloader the chances of actually hitting anything, especially those pesky-ass crows, really wasn't very good.

He hadn't cared if he'd brought home meat for the stew pot, though. His best memories of those hunting parties had always been tramping through the woods with Danny and his dad and listening to his old man's stories. One thing was for certain, Joshua Mackay, could spin a tail like none other.

And those stories really were the reason Ian and Danny had enlisted in the Marines less than a week after their high school graduation.

But then Danny hadn't joined the Marines with him just because of the stories or because they were the best friends in the whole world. He'd enlisted first and foremost because Joshua Mackay expected it of him, just as much as he'd expected it of Ian. And Danny wasn't one to ever disappoint Joshua Mackay.

He'd been like a second son to Ian's father, especially since he'd had no real father of his own to speak of. And over the years, he'd spent more nights, weekends, holidays, and summer vacations at Ian's house than he ever spent at his own.

Danny had always been the one who at least acted like he was interested in the farming side of Joshua Mackay's life, even though he really wasn't, just to take the pressure off his friend's shoulders.

Ian hung his head and sighed.

There'd been times when he'd wondered if, given the choice, his father would've preferred it'd been Danny who came home from Afghanistan, instead of him. He really couldn't have blamed him if he had.

There were times he wished that very same thing himself.

Yes, Joshua Mackay had been a good father and a good man, and he'd deserved better in a son than what he'd gotten. He'd deserved someone who couldn't wait to follow in his footsteps, someone who would've been proud to work the land and serve his country at the same time. Someone who hadn't gotten Danny, the son of his heart, killed.

But had Joshua Mackay gotten any of that?

No, he hadn't.

All he'd ever gotten for his hard work, dedication, and sacrifice had been a broken shell of a worthless sack of shit son when it was all said and done.

But was there some way, even four hundred years in the past, to make up for the mistakes he'd made in that life? And not just the death of Danny and his men, but so many other things he wished he'd done differently?

Only one thing came to mind.

He could stop thinking only of himself and his mistakes and give Aila and this Ian Mackay's child the kind of father his own father had been to him. Even if that meant staying in this time period longer than he'd planned.

A smile broke out on his face for the first time since leaving Borve castle.

He could teach a son to take pride in his country and his land. To protect his loved ones to his last breath and to provide for all those under his care. And if the child were a girl? He'd help Aila guide their daughter into womanhood as gently as possible. But he'd also make sure any daughter of his was as tough as any boy and just as resilient. No one would make his daughter feel like she wasn't good enough just because she'd been born female.

But then what of Danny and the other men he'd lost that day in Afghanistan? Would they mind waiting a little while longer for him to relive that day? Probably not. Especially since none of them would even be a gleam in their fathers' eyes for close to four hundred years yet.

Fate had told him it was up to him how long he stayed in the past and when he was ready to return to that particular day in Afghanistan. But today wasn't that day, or tomorrow either, or anytime in the foreseeable future. He had a life here with Aila to pursue, a family on the way, people who counted on him to be their laird, and a chance to do it right this time.

With his mind made up, Ian put his back into the tedious job of mining the sulfur he needed for the black powder. Fergus Gordon was coming. Of that Ian had no doubt. And come hell-or-high-water, this Ian Mackay was going to be here to stop him.

****

It was the strangest thing, the sudden absence of sound that startled her awake.

Well, the sudden absence of old Brody's snoring really.

At first, Aila hadn't been able to sleep because of the racket, and now she couldn't imagine the comfort of that particular sound not being there as she drifted off to peaceful slumber. That sound meant safety. The sound meant she wasn't alone, that he was watching over her, even if he was just a crotchety old fisherman.

Aila chuckled. Yes, Brody Mackay was very much

a crotchety old fisherman, that's for sure. She'd learned to appreciate that about him.

Over the last couple of fortnights, since Ian had been gone, she and Brody had spent many turns of the hourglass together simply talking. He'd taught her so much about the art of fishing, and she'd taught him how to treat minor wounds his men might encounter while out at sea. They'd gone for long walks, picked late summer berries, argued about any and everything, and more than anything else, they'd laughed.

He'd become so important to her. Certainly, more than a body guard or just a companion while Ian had been away. He'd become more like the father she'd never known. And she loved him for it, truly she did, foul-fish breath, loud snores, and all.

But then who wouldn't love old Brody? The entire Mackay clan did, that was for sure.

She strained to listen and smiled into the darkness. The old man had probably just needed to go relieve himself and would be back any moment now. Any healer worth their salt kenned with age came a more frequent need to empty the body of its fluids. If one were lucky that is.

Perhaps she ought to brew up an elixir for the old man, a combination of ground ginger and celery, with perhaps some dried beets and fresh blueberries thrown in for good measure. That'd get him pissing a healthy stream.

She giggled to herself. All these thoughts about the process and need for peeing had that same urge now affecting her.

Quickly, she rose and wrapped a fur about her shoulders for warmth. If she hurried, she could probably even beat Brody back and he'd never know she'd been out of her room.

She rushed to the door, threw it wide open, and stumbled over a limp body at her feet.

Aila gasped.

There lay Brody Mackay, lead fisherman for the clan Mackay, her personal bodyguard and dear friend, with his eyes wide open but no longer seeing. He was dead, stone cold dead, with a dagger sunk hilt-deep in his chest.

And not just any dagger either, but a blade bearring the family crest of the clan Gordon.

But Brody wasn't alone in death. It appeared the old man had fought his attacker valiantly and had managed to find purchase for his own weapon. Lachlan Gordon, her first cousin, her first kiss, and not to mention, one of Fergus's most trusted allies, lay marinating in a pool of his own blood.

Aila dropped to her knees, gently cradled old Brody's head in her lap, and screamed.

Chapter Seventeen

Late October 1643
Borve Castle

He'd been home for almost a sennight and still couldn't believe Brody Mackay had been really and truly dead for more than two fortnights and was buried up on the hill overlooking his precious sea.

Ian grimaced. A month, almost a frigging month, not two fortnights.

When had he begun thinking of time in measures of fortnights instead of the two-week period the word fortnight stood for? And when was the last time he'd even thought in terms of days and hours or minutes and seconds? Perhaps he really was becoming a seventeenth century Highlander, after all.

There'd been a time in his life when knowing exactly what time it was, to the very second had been imperative to his well-being and to the well-being of his men. Not just time, but distance, too.

While the drop rate of a mortar shell was less than three seconds, one click was and always would be a thousand meters. And then, of course, there were map coordinates and compass bearings, scope calibrations to the millionth power, morning strategy meetings at a specific hour, and nighttime guard duty for hours upon end. And on and on and on while in Afghanistan.

But in 1643 Scotland, even though they had

hourglasses, time was measured more often in seasons, or where the sun happened to be on any given day, or how empty one's belly felt. And distance was totally random, too. Like "that field over the rise. Ye ken which one I mean, do ye nae?" Or "old Argus's place over on the coast by that really big rock." Or "that one berry patch with those really sweet berries. Ye ken where I'm talking aboot?"

And now he needed to add his own Scottish directions to those of his kinsmen. For it was imperative that no Mackay be caught in a trap meant for a Gordon.

Fergus might have started this fight by forcing that stupid promise on Aila in the first place and then by sending his man to try and harm her and their unborn child, but killing Brody had been the last straw. And Ian planned on finishing this fight before Fergus ever got another chance.

He'd thought the trip to Tongue would never end. Day after fucking day of digging and collecting the precious sulfur while always being on the lookout for Mackays, Gordons, and even Sutherlands who weren't part of Stephen's particular clan.

He'd even gone so far as to don a plain non-descript kilt, so he wouldn't garner suspicion. It had been one of the solid mud color ones the fisherman were so fond of wearing. For no fisherman worth his salt would dare chance getting nasty-ass fish guts on his clan's kilt. It'd been Brody who'd loaned Ian the garment.

Damn, he really missed that old man.

Ian shook his head. He couldn't worry about Brody right now, though. He needed to concentrate on problems he could do something about.

Since returning from Tongue, he'd made up a few batches of the black powder. And he'd already put most of it to good use. The clan Mackay was now the proud owner of a stockpile of primitive grenades he'd personally fashioned from the powder, mud, and strips of old plaid dipped in whale oil. There were more than a dozen well-thought-out traps laid all along the borders between Mackay and Sutherland lands to boot.

Some of those traps were filled with enough black powder to completely blow a man's head off his shoulders while others were simply holes in the ground wide enough and deep enough to really piss off whoever happened to find themselves stuck at the bottom of one. Some had sharp spikes to rip the skin and break the bones, and some were laced with enough smelly pig shit to make Daniel happy and any stranger think twice about trying to advance farther onto Mackay land where he wasn't welcome.

Each and every trap had been carefully planned and crafted with only one thing in mind. Make Fergus Gordon pay for frightening his wife and killing his friend.

Every time he glanced toward the sea, he expected to see the trusted, old fisherman walking the deck of his ship, issuing orders, unfurling sails, and telling stories. But today, just like the previous week since he'd gotten home, there was no Brody in sight, and there never would be again.

Fuck, fuck, fuck, fuck, fuck!

It wasn't as if he could afford to be a good man down right now either, especially a man like Brody. And it sure as hell wasn't a good time for a war with Aila's fucking brother.

It was fall in this northern most part of Scotland and past time to finish the harvest. The survival of his clan depended upon bringing in every grain, vegetable, and fruit to be found and putting them safely in the cellar alongside the bounty of the sea that old Brody had helped supply them with. The cod, salmon, and halibut, along with the crab and lobster, whale and seal. It had all been salted and dried, and now sat right beside where the wild game hung.

Herbs were already drying, and the clan, as a whole, was well on its way to being prepared for the coming winter. At least they had been before work all but stopped in order to get ready for the arrival of Fergus Gordon and his bunch.

Even most of the whisky had been brewed and the ale barreled, and Ian hoped desperately they'd get to enjoy every last drop over the next few months.

And then there was still the ongoing problem with Aila.

What the hell was he going to do about his very sad pregnant wife? Brody's death and how it had happened had affected her deeply.

No longer was she carefree and happy. She didn't laugh or even smile very often anymore. As a matter of fact, more often than not those beautiful green eyes of hers were red rimmed, and her demeanor darkly somber. Rarely did she utter a word anymore, especially to him. And when she did speak, her utterances were more often than not meant for the ears of the cook or for whatever ailing clansman she happened to be treating that day.

But when she did glance his way, when she did manage a word meant for his ears, her voice usually trembled, and her eyes filled with unshed tears and guilt, so much guilt. As if she'd somehow convinced herself that she could've prevented Brody's death by simply not breathing anymore herself.

It was silly. She couldn't have stopped what happened.

But what could he do to bring her out of her funk? Holding her tightly, kissing her gently, stoking her fire while bringing her to climax with his fingers and tongue certainly hadn't helped much or for very long.

Ian kicked himself for his lack of experience with women.

In his time, a guy brought a girl flowers or candy to make her smile, jewelry if he could afford it. But this was 1643 Scotland and Aila wasn't some silly little chit who could be easily talked out of her gloom with pretties.

But then she had legitimate reason to be worried, too, didn't she? After all, her own dickhead of a brother had sworn to kill her.

Perhaps he couldn't make everything all right all the time. And perhaps he couldn't solve every problem they'd ever have in their lifetime together. But there was one problem he could start solving tonight. They hadn't truly made love since he'd gotten back because he was trying to give her time and space and comfort in order to come to terms with what had happened. But he missed that beautiful smile, and it was past time to put it back on both their faces, and hopefully for longer than a little while this time.

So what if he didn't have bouquets of flowers to give her, or candy or jewels. He had himself, and he'd love that smile back where it belonged if it was the last thing he ever did.

****

Aila paced her chamber.

If she wasn't such a coward, she'd pack the few belongings she owned and leave this place this very moment. Ian—and these people, this clan—who had taken her in and accepted her without question or reservation were all in danger, and it was her fault. If she was no longer here, perhaps he'd just leave them alone.

Fergus had no cause ta be angry with any of them.

Not that that would matter when he showed up at Borve Castle. For he would. And though Ian was certain his traps would stop him, Aila kenned better.

When Fergus finally made his way past Ian's traps and black powder, his anger would be taken out on the young and the old, men, women, and children alike. Even though it had been her and only her who'd broken the promise to him.

She paced faster.

It should've been her who'd paid the price in the first place, not Brody. If her life had been forfeited instead, then this would've already been long over with.

Aila ran her hand over her expanding belly and fear threatened to take her breath away. Not the babe, though. God please not the babe. The bairn was innocent in all of this. Surly Fergus could be convinced of that, couldn't he?

Even as the thought crossed her mind, she knew the futility of it. Fergus had never been one to listen to a word she had to say. He'd only ever made demands of her and had expected his dictates to be followed without question. Dictates she could not and would not follow this time.

Her motherly instincts were much more powerful than her fear, however. And those instincts were screaming for her to run. Run as far away and as fast from this place as she could get. But that thought didn't set right with her either.

Run away from Ian? Leave him here to face the anger of Fergus alone? She could nae. She loved him too much to do that.

And these people? Leave the Mackays to the mercy of the Gordons? No, they were her clan now, her family, her responsibility. She'd not do it. She couldn't.

But then, if she couldn't leave and she couldn't stay, what could she do? Perhaps she should leave it up to her husband or at least give him the option of separating himself from what was to come. If he wanted her to leave, she would. It would break her heart into a million pieces, but she'd do it.

A moment later, every single thought she'd just been thinking faded into the background as Ian walked into their room with a handful of wilted heather, of all things, and held it out toward her with a shy smile on his much too handsome face. "I know they're not as pretty as you, especially this time of year, but it's all I could think of to make you smile. I miss your smile, Aila. I miss it a lot."

It was the most beautiful gesture she'd ever seen, and her eyes filled with tears.

"No, no, no, don't cry, my love," Ian whispered as he gathered her into his arms. "The last thing I ever want to do is make you cry."

She sniffed. "Ye just make me so verra happy Ian, and I've brought nae but trouble down upon ye and yer people. Ye should nae be bringing me anything, ye daft man. Ye should be sending me and the bairn packing for the clan's sake."

The man chuckled and the sound of it, the feel of it against her skin brought a small smile to Aila's face, too.

"I'll not be sending you or our child anywhere that I'm not. And neither will anyone else in this clan. You are their lady." He patted her expanding belly. "And he is their future laird."

She placed her hands on both sides of his face and forced him to look her straight in the eye. "Do nae ye understand? With me gone, there could be a new lady, one who would nae bring trouble along with her. And brand new bairns whose blood would nae be half Gordon."

He took her hands in his, brought them to his lips, and gently kissed them. "You're the only woman this heart wants and will ever need. I love you, and I love our child, and I'm not willing to give either one of you up, ever. Fuck Fergus Gordon. The Mackays will stand together against him if and when it comes to that. Every last one of us, and that's all there is to it."

She started to speak again, but her words were lost as his lips captured hers in a kiss that shattered her resistance. Heat flooded her as tendrils of excitement skittered along her spine landing deep in the pit of her belly. It'd been too long since he'd been deep inside her, and she simply couldn't resist his touch, his taste, the feel of his body up against hers.

Of their own volition, her arms wrapped around his neck, and a deep sigh of contentment mingled with one of his own.

"Ian, I need..." she whispered.

He lifted her into his arms and carried her toward their bed. "We both need," he whispered back a moment before he covered her body with his own.

It was heaven, the weight and the heat of him in and all around her. She smiled. Ian was right. They did need this.

Tears threatened, and she fought them back. Not today, not here, not now. There was no telling what pain the coming days would bring, but for this day, for this moment in time, with this man whom she loved with all her heart, there was no place for tears. Tomorrow, she'd cry if she had to.

Slowly, he rocked her from the inside out, and she met each thrust with eager anticipation as her body melded with his, adding its own give and take to the dance they shared. Then he kissed first her lips and nuzzled her neck before capturing a pert nipple between his teeth and gently nipping.

Spasms of pure pleasure shot straight through her cunny, and Aila gasped. It wasn't even a heartbeat later that she heard his shout above her and felt the warmth of his climax filling her. Though she missed both the warmth and the weight of him as he pulled out and snuggled up against her, she couldn't help but smile and sigh contently.

Being a wife to this man was heaven. This was the way marriage should be. One man, one woman sharing both the good times and bad. It was on the tip of her tongue to beg him to do what he had just done all over again when the sound of an explosion somewhere in the distance suddenly erupted.

"What the hell?" Ian jumped up, grabbed his kilt

and sword, and headed for the door. A heartbeat before he got to it, though, he turned back around towards her. "Stay here. It sounds like your brother just may have arrived for his uninvited visit."

Aila had no intentions of staying where she was told. That was her husband, her heart, heading out to meet God only knew how many angry Gordons, and like it or not, he wasn't going alone.

As quickly as possible, she dressed in order to follow him. Before she could even get to the door of the keep, it swung wide open and in strode Rhona, her very angry looking sister by marriage, whose face was covered with soot and whose dress was in tatters. To make matters worse, she was bellowing like a banshee.

"Ye just wait till Fergus finds oot someone tried ta blow his wife ta pieces. Crazy Mackays, the lot of them, I tell ye. And if trying ta blow up his wife wasn't bad enough, they tried ta blow up the woman who's carrying his bairn. And why? Just because she came a callin' on his sister? Ye just wait till he hears aboot it. He won't be at all happy. I can tell ye that."

Chapter Eighteen

Ian ran his fingers through his hair and took a deep calming breath to make sure he didn't yell at his very pregnant sister-in-law like he so desperately wanted to. "Like I've already told you ten times at least, I was not trying to kill you. At least not precisely you."

"Ye almost killed my horse," Rhona sobbed. "And ye verra well could've killed me and my bairn."

What was it about a weeping woman that could bring a grown man to his knees every single time? Not just Rhona either, but Aila was sniffling right along with her. And not just sniffling but tearing up and her lower lip was trembling in a most adorable fashion. Then there was old Agnes the cook, who was fawning over both Aila and Rhona while swiping tears from her own eyes with her grease-covered sleeve and glaring right at him as if he'd committed the crime of the century.

God help him. If he didn't do something to get control of this conversation soon, he'd have an entire keep full of blathering females on his hands. But what could one man do?

"And all I wanted was ta visit with me sister and ask Aila if she'd be good enough ta attend me when the bairn comes," Rhona wailed. "What else could I do since ye took her so far away from us? We nae have a healer of our own anymore, ye ken." She sobbed again.

"Fergus told me nae ta come here. Even told me I could nae on fear of his anger, but I did nae listen. He said a Mackay was never born who could be trusted. I did nae believe him then. I do now."

Ian opened his mouth to respond, but Rhona wasn't anywhere close to being done. "And ye did nae just almost kill me horse and almost kill me and the bairn, and the two Gordon men traveling with me, but now it looks as if ye mean ta kill any Gordon who dares step on Mackay land? Even me poor, unsuspecting, innocent Fergus, the father of me unborn child and yer wife's verra own brither, when he dares come visiting his self? Shame on ye, Ian Mackay. Shame on yer black heart."

Rhona wailed once more. "Ye are a monster, a true monster, I tell ye. For only such an evil creature such as ye would do as ye've done and dig holes of death for yer fellow man ta fall inta instead of having the honor and decency of meeting a man ye have a problem with face ta face on the field of battle. If'n I did nae ken your linage, I'd swear ye ta be…English."

Aila gasped as if slapped, and old Agnes sputtered and choked, as if the very thought of being considered English was the worst possible insult anyone could ever level.

Ian had had enough. "That trap was more noise than anything else, and you know it. Other than being spooked, neither you nor your horse, nor your two guardsmen are any worse for the wear."

"And poor innocent Fergus?

"You've gotta be kidding me. There isn't anything innocent about your husband, my lady. He has sent spies to this keep. He's threatened the life of my wife and my child. And he got a good man killed. If he does dare to step a foot on Mackay land, I'll make sure he regrets it."

Rhona stomped her foot. "If he steps foot on Mackay land? Of course, he's going ta be stepping foot on Mackay land. He's nae doubt on his way as we speak. After all, I'm here, aren't I? Where his wife and child is so will he be eventually. And why do ye think he'd threaten Aila? She's his sister. He'd nae ever hurt her. He did nae do anything that ever got anyone killed, at least nae lately." She turned toward the woman she'd just been talking about. "You tell him, Aila. Tell yer daft husband he's wrong aboot our Fergus."

Suddenly, Rhona grabbed her large belly, bent over, and moaned.

Aila wrapped her arm around Rhona's waist, gently helped her into a chair, then glared at Ian. "Now look what ye've done."

"Me," he yelled.

"Yes, ye," she yelled back at him. "Our sister is heavy with child, and ye have distressed her and continue ta do so. Instead of raising yer voice ta a poor innocent mam ta be, perhaps ye could be of use and help me get her upstairs ta our room so she can rest. She's traveled far."

Ian sighed but kept his mouth shut.

Their room? Just fucking great.

Not only did he have to open their home to his enemy's wife, but it appeared he would have to give her his bed to boot. He didn't voice that complaint, however. He knew better. Even if he hadn't been outnumbered three to one, it didn't take a genius to know baby in the belly trumped husband in the bed any day of the week.

"Oh, and when we've gotten her settled," Aila continued, "ye'll be undoing those traps ye set. I ken yer concerns aboot Fergus, truly I do. But ye'll just have ta find another way, husband. For I'll nae have Rhona so worried that this bairn comes even one day before he's meant ta."

****

Aila paced back and forth before the window in her chamber and stared down at the bailey in hopes of catching a glimpse of Ian. He probably thought she'd lost her mind. After all, one moment she'd been completely in agreement with him and his plans for protecting them all, and then she simply could not.

It had been the fear and pain in Rhona's eyes that changed her mind. That and the fact that even to protect herself and her child, she could never live with the fact she'd been responsible for the death of her brother. There had to be another way. There simply had to be.

Ian was a smart man. Surely, he could come up with something less lethal? Something that would change Fergus's mind but would not stress poor Rhona ta the point of delivering early. Not that she was that far off right now. If the size of her belly was any indication she probably only had about a sennight or so ta go.

"When should yer bairn be coming?" Rhona asked.

In the excitement of the last few hours, Aila had forgotten that Fergus probably hadn't told Rhona about the fact she was also carrying. Especially if the man had planned on the child never drawing a breath. Not that she could say that to Rhona, though.

"Umm, probably right after Hogmanay," is what she settled for.

Rhona smiled. "That's a fine proper way ta start the

new year and a family. I've always been partial ta celebrating the Hogmanay meself. I liked the first footing best. Me da was always first one welcomed inta everyone's homes because he was verra dark headed, ye ken. And the food..." She smiled even wider. "The black bun, the shortbread, the rabbit, and venison. Oh, and the clootie dumplin' with custard sauce. Me mouth waters just thinking aboot it."

Suddenly, Rhona became serious. "So ye are happy then, Aila? With yer Mackay husband and these strange people? He seems a little titched in the head if'n ye ask me. All these dangerous holes in the ground that he calls traps and such. And his crazy talk aboot Fergus. What nonsense that he'd think our Fergus would ever hurt ye."

Aila swallowed hard. "I am happy, very happy. And ye do nae ken Ian the way I do. He is a good man and verra protective of me, of all his people."

She took a deep breath in order to give herself the chance to think of how to word what needed to be said without upsetting Rhona too much. "After the wedding Fergus said some hateful things, made threats." She held up a hand when it looked like Rhona would respond. "I ken he was well inta his cups and sometimes says things he does nae mean, but he made serious threats, Rhona. And then after Lachlan did what he did, what else were we ta think?"

"Lachlan? Lachlan Gordon, yer cousin? What did he do?" Rhona asked.

Aila sat on the edge of the bed and took her sister by marriage's hand in her own. "He killed Brody, a dear friend who was watching over me while Ian was away. He did it right outside this verra door while I was sleeping where ye now lay."

"So where is Lachlan now if he did such a thing," Rhona gasped. "Did yer husband kill him outright or lock him away somewhere?"

Aila shook her head. "Nae, Lachlan lost his own life while taking Brody Mackay's. That's how we kenned it was him."

"Oh my." Rhona sighed. "So that's why yer husband is so angry with mine then. He thinks Fergus sent Lachlan, does he nae?"

All Aila could do was nod.

Rhona bit her lip. "I should probably warn ye that yer brither may nae be too hospitable-like when he does finally arrive."

Dread filled Aila. "And just why should he nae be?"

Rhona swallowed. "He out right forbade me ta come, but I did nae listen. And ye ken full well Fergus does nae take kindly ta being disobeyed. I waited until he was off visiting the Sutherland, ye ken, and then I snuck off in the middle of the night with only the two guardsmen at my side. Aye, he's nae gonna be happy at all."

Aila gulped. Oh great, Fergus wasn't going to be happy, and Ian already wasn't. She almost wished there was somewhere she could run off to.

****

Ian was beyond pissed. He was livid.

It had taken three full sun ups till sun downs to undo all the hard work he had put into those stupid traps. Three backbreaking days of slowly emptying and refilling each and every fucking hole while making sure he didn't blow up himself or any of his men while he was at it. And all the while keeping an eye out for the two Gordon guardsmen, so he didn't give away Mackay secrets, let alone watching for Fergus to arrive.

And why?

Because his pretty little pregnant, hormonal wife, and his even more pregnant, more hormonal sister-in-law had him firmly by the short-and-curlies, and they both knew it. How was it females were born with the innate knowledge that all they need do in order to get their way with a man was bat their eyes, look all innocent-like, and turn on the water works?

Well, it wasn't going to work, not anymore. No, sir, it certainly wasn't. And as soon as he stored this last bag of black powder safely in the back of the blacksmith's shed, he was going to tell them both that.

Granted, he had reluctantly done as Aila asked and taken all the traps apart. Unfortunately, Fergus wouldn't be getting his useless ass blown up any time soon. At least not by the traps anyway, but that didn't mean Ian didn't still have his stash of makeshift hand grenades close by.

That thought made him smile.

Just let Rhona's dear ole husband step one foot onto Mackay land and make one more threat toward his wife, and see if he didn't shove one of those handy-dandy grenades right up Fergus's big, fat, hairy highlander ass and light it. Claymore-swinging crazy barbarian or not, Ian wasn't going to take any more chances when it came to Aila's or their child's safety, and she was just going to have to understand that about him.

Not that she cared one wit what he thought about anything right now anyway.

The blasted woman hadn't spoken more than a hand full of words to him in days, and then only in passing. Most of her time was spent rubbing Rhona's back or seeing to Rhona's meals or checking Rhona's belly or any other number of Rhona related tasks she'd taken upon herself.

And during all this time where had Ian been? That was, when he hadn't been out breaking his back, dismantling traps, and seeing to every other need of their people? He hadn't even been allowed to sleep at his wife's side since his sister-in-law arrived. Rhona Gordon was firmly ensconced right in the middle of his bed.

Oh no, he had been relegated to the cold, hard floor of the keep, right alongside every other male Mackay inhabitant of Borve castle unfortunate enough not to have a wife. He was so angry, so frustrated, that he almost didn't hear Daniel's panicked shouts, and it took him a moment to realize exactly what the little boy was yelling.

"Laird," Daniel wheezed as he came to a halt in front of him, bent forward to catch his breath, then looked back up. "There be an angry looking Sutherland riding this-a way. A really, really big one, and he's moving fast."

Ian placed a hand on the lad's shoulder. He might be gearing up for battle, but the last thing he wanted to do was frighten the child. "I'm pretty sure that's not a Sutherland but your lady's brother, a Gordon, finally come to fetch his wife." Then he winked. "Though, in truth, I doubt there's much difference between the two."

A moment later, the form of Fergus Gordon broke through a small copse of trees from the north. True to

Daniel's observations, on first inspection, it appeared the man was riding alone, though Ian doubted it. Why would the laird of a large clan travel unaccompanied into his enemy's camp without so much as a single guardsman to watch his back? No sane highlander, if anyone could consider Fergus Gordon anywhere near sane, would do such a thing.

Ian scanned the horizon for more heads to pop up and braced himself for the upcoming confrontation. A part of him was glad the waiting was finally over. It was well past time to put an end to the threats against his family, whether his wife and sister-in-law liked it or not.

His hand was firmly on the hilt of his claymore when the horse came to a sudden jarring halt at his feet. Its owner jumped down and squarely faced him a mere moment before the man's legs began to wobble, and Fergus Gordon dropped to his knees.

"Me wife, Rhona, she's here. Aye?" he asked with a shaky voice not much louder than a whisper. "Tell me she is, man," he pleaded. "And tell me she and me bairn be safe."

Ian almost felt sorry for him…almost. He knew very well, since having a wife of his own, how a woman could drive a man to the very brink of insanity and back again. But that didn't mean he wasn't also going to enjoy his enemy's discomfort for at least a moment. After all, he had it coming for threatening Aila.

He smiled.

Poor Fergus looked ready to pass out from exhaustion. His words were coming in quick little spurts, his limbs visibly shaking, and it was obvious the man was having a hard time trying to catch his breath. If truth be told, his horse didn't look much better than he did. The man obviously had rode the poor thing full out without stopping from his castle to this one.

For the space of one heartbeat, he thought about telling Fergus he hadn't seen hide-nor-hair of Rhona Gordon, but he couldn't. The look in the man's eyes, the pain, the fear, was something Ian knew too well.

"Aye, she's here, and they're both safe." He nodded and held out a hand. "Let me help you up, and I'll take you to them." Then, for just a second, he pulled the hand back. "But if you dare try and harm my wife, my child, I'll kill you myself. Do we understand each other?"

A look of confusion came over Fergus Gordon's face as he took hold of Ian's once more outstretched arm. "Harm yer wife? Why in God's name would I harm yer wife, me verra own sister? It's me wife I'm gonna kill as soon as I get me hands on her."

Chapter Nineteen

"What do ye mean I cannae see me wife?"

Aila stood at the base of the stairs with her hands on her hips and glared at her brother. "I mean, ye'll nae be climbing these stairs or stepping a foot further inta Castle Borve until a few things have been settled between the two of us."

He glared back at her. "Why ye mean stubborn little wench. Why is it ye always have ta be this way? For just once in yer life, could ye nae be a pain in me arse and simply do as ye are told?"

She shook her head and protectively placed her arms across the top of her expanding belly. Tears threatened, but she fought them off. It wouldn't do to let Fergus see he'd wounded her. The laird of clan Gordon was well known for taking advantage of his adversary's weaknesses, and she had no intention of letting him see hers.

"I am nae the mean one," she said. "Ye are. I've been seeing ta the welfare of yer bairn while ye've been planning the death of mine. And I'm here ta tell ye that I'm nae having it. We will live in peace or I'll…I'll…" She stomped her foot. "I'll kill ye meself."

The man had the audacity to grin and chuckle. "Aila, we both ken ye'd nae even kill a bug let alone yer brither so ye can just stop with all the bluster. And what is this nonsense about yer bairn? Why would ye think such a thing of me? Did yer useless Mackay husband put such thoughts into yer head? 'Cause if he did…" Fergus fisted both his hands, and the grin he'd had a moment ago faded into a scowl.

Before she even realized what she was about to do, Aila delivered a quick, right jab to his nose, and the startled look on Fergus's face was almost worth the worry she'd been putting herself through since Rhona's arrival. "Why would I think such a thing?"

She almost punched him again, but this time he caught her hand before it could make contact, brought it to his lips, and kissed it tenderly.

She struggled for a moment to free herself but couldn't, and the tears she'd been holding at bay overflowed her eyes and slid silently down her cheeks. "Nae, me husband did nae put such thoughts in me head, brither. It was ye. Ye've hated me since the day I was born, and I ken it. And after the wedding, during our dance, ye said if I dared give Ian an heir, ye'd make sure it never drew a breath and do nae deny it now."

He dropped her hand, turned, slowly walked over to the great table, sat down heavily, and gestured for her and Ian both to join him. "Do ye perhaps have a dram or two of whisky ta spare? I'm right parched, and I do believe this conversation is gonna warrant some long before we're through."

It took no more than a handful of minutes for one of old Agnes's granddaughters to deliver the desired tankard of whisky to Fergus and one of ale to both Ian and Aila. To Aila, it seemed like forever.

Before Fergus had even finished his first sip, she was right back at him. "Well? Now that ye've been given repast, what do ye have ta say fer yerself?"

Fergus sighed and set his tankard down with a loud clunk. "I do nae hate ye. I never have. Ye are me sister. A true pain in me arse ta be sure, but me sister just the same. I do nae remember saying such an awful thing ta ye on the day ye married. Nae that it's an excuse, but I was well inta me cups by then and could've said anything. But if I did truly say such a thing, I am sorry." He stood and glared down at her. "Now may I see me wife?"

She stood and faced him toe-to-toe. "That's all ye have ta say? Ye do nae remember because ye were blootered?"

Fergus nodded. "Aye? What else is there?"

He turned toward Ian. "Can ye nae explain ta yer wife what it's like when a man is well inta his cups? For ye certainly have been many times."

Suddenly, Fergus's eyes narrowed. "At least the Ian Mackay I knew never missed an opportunity ta down a whisky, yet here ye set sipping ale like a lass? And that little serving wench who brought drink ta the table... Ye didn't so much as look her way once, let alone grab her arse or a teet or even plop her in yer lap for a little slap and tickle. Has marriage to me sister cut off yer balls, then? I ken she is difficult at best, but I did nae ken she'd so easily unman a Mackay." He chuckled. "Perhaps the Gordons have been doing this feud thing all wrong and should've sent our women folk against ye ta begin with."

Ian stood and met Fergus glare for glare.

Worry filled Aila as she tried desperately to distract her brother from his current train of thought, and her husband from his rising anger. "Did ye nae say ye wanted ta see yer wife, Fergus? Well, what are ye waiting for, then?"

But it was as if Fergus hadn't even heard her and just kept talking to Ian. "I did nae really believe it when me men returned and told me ye'd changed yer drinking, fighting, whoring ways, but now I wonder. Just who are ye, and what have ye done with the Ian Mackay I kenned so well? Ye look like him, but ye do nae act like him at all."

Ian balled up his fists. "When your men returned? So you admit you've been sending spies to Borve Castle then."

Aila placed herself directly between her husband and her brother, a hand on each man's chest. "Now is nae the time. Ye can kill each other later."

Ian opened his mouth to say something else but never got the chance as a shout from above stopped them all in their tracks. "Aila, come quick," Rhona cried. "I fear the bairn's decided he's nae waiting any longer."

Fergus turned toward the stairs while shouting over his shoulder. "Find the two guardsmen that came with me wife and tell them ta saddle the horses and be ready ta ride as soon as I gather her up."

Aila grabbed his arm and would've been pulled along behind him if Ian hadn't somehow managed to step in front of Fergus and stop his forward motion.

"What are you thinking, man? You can't pluck up your pregnant wife and just ride off into the sunset with her. Think about what you're doing. She's about to give birth."

"I ken exactly what I'm doing, ye bloody bastard," Fergus yelled. "Nae Gordon heir is gonna be born on Mackay land. Especially nae my son."

Aila punched him right between his shoulder blades. "Would ye rather yer bairn be born alive here or dead somewhere down the road, 'cause that's exactly what's gonna happen if ye try and move her now. And ye could lose yer wife in the bargain ta boot."

It was like all the air suddenly went out of Fergus. He sat down heavily and put his face in his hands. "Aye, ye are right. Do what ye can, please, sister. But God help me, I do nae ken how I'm ever gonna explain ta me people or the Sutherlands how the new Gordon laird-ta-be, came ta be born on stinking Mackay land, in a stinking Mackay castle, in a stinking Mackay bed, and birthed by a stinking Mackay healer. Even if that healer is me verra own sister."

He closed his eyes and placed his hands together in prayer. "Though I can nae believe I'm asking this of ye, Lord. Let this one bairn be a lass, please, I beg of ye. Nae one will care where a lass was born, ye ken?"

Aila patted him on the shoulder while smiling up at Ian. "Take me brither back ta the stinking Mackay high table, please, before I do kill him. Give the man another dram or two of stinking Mackay whisky ta ease his tender little Gordon worries while I see ta helping me sister bring his bairn, be it lass or laddie, safely inta this world.

"And if ye do nae mind, have ole Agnes feed the man some stinking Mackay food. He looks near ready ta pass oot, and I do nae have time ta be tending ta his stinking old arse right now. Stinking Mackay healer that I am and all."

****

"God, she's a stubborn little wench. Always has been." Fergus yawned loudly, then burped and farted just before raising his fifth tankard of Castle Borve's *uisge beatha* to his lips and taking a big swallow.

Ian shook his head. The sun was just beginning to rise, and it had been hours since Aila climbed those stairs to help deliver the baby and left him all alone at the great table with her idiot brother. Hour after endless hour of listening to Fergus Gordon fluctuate between snoring and ranting about his sister and the evils of Mackays in general.

"It's nae me fault she's the way she is either, I tell ya. I did the best I could ta raise her right. But would she ever listen ta me counsel? Nae. Not even once. I should've beat her. That's what I should've done fer sure." Fergus burped again.

This time Ian did almost say something, but the sight of a very tired looking Aila slowing making her way down the steps stopped him. Instead, he simply watched her as she smiled shyly and sat down on the very last step.

"I could nae ever beat her though," Fergus continued. "Even though she needed it many times, ta be sure. But she was nae bigger than a rabbit the day me mam placed her in me arms, ye ken. And right before me mam died, she made me promise ta take care of Aila and ta always protect her. I gave me mam me word."

Fergus shook his head and just continued to shake it as if trying to come to terms with something Ian wasn't so sure he wanted to hear. But it was obvious Aila's brother was in a talkative mood and nothing was going to prevent him from saying whatever it was he felt Ian needed to hear.

"I did nae ken anything about caring fer a lass. Not

that we did nae have a wet nurse for her 'cause we did. But then me da died, too, and I was suddenly laird on top of being Aila's protector. I did nae ken what ta do with her. I was but thirteen summers, ye ken, and she was so small, so trusting, so damn stubborn and willful from the verra day she was born." His voice rose an octave. "I swear, the older that lass got the more stubborn and willful she became."

Ian listened to Fergus's words, but it was Aila whom he was watching and couldn't help but smile a little himself as her brother's words caused her pretty little lips to curve slightly upward.

"I bet she was a stubborn little thing," he said to Fergus while winking at Aila. Her smile grew even bigger.

"Aye, she was," Fergus continued, "and I could nae keep me promise ta me mam nae matter how hard I tried. That lass was always taking chances she did nae have ta take, ye ken. Climbing where nae lass ever need climb. Scaring the verra life out of me. Acting more like a lad than any lass had a right ta.

"She kenned nae fear, I'll tell ye. She'd run right inta a fire if someone did nae stop her. She'd run right inta a dwelling filled with the sick too. I cannae tell ye how many times I locked her in her room ta keep her safe, but it did nae good. Willful, willful lass." he sighed. "Damn, stubborn, willful lass, but God help me, I love her. She's me only true blood family. At least before Rhona came along that is."

He suddenly looked Ian straight in the eye, and Ian returned his stare. "It almost killed me ta have ta give her ta ye. She deserved better than a Mackay, especially one the likes of ye. I cannae tell ye how many men wanted ta take her ta wife. How many offers fer her hand I had. But I could nae ever be sure any of them would make her happy, so I denied them all, nae matter what they offered. Nae man was good enough fer me sister, and certainly nae ye."

Ian couldn't seem to help himself. He had to ask. "Not even Lachlan?"

Fergus actually laughed, and for a moment, it was all Ian could do not to punch him right in the nose.

"Lachlan Gordon? Why would ye think I'd ever give me only sister ta the likes of that pissant?" He chuckled again. "Oh, he wanted her fer sure, but there's a mean streak down deep in Lachlan. I'd nae give him a dog let alone me sister. I would've hated ta have had ta kill me own cousin." Fergus grinned widely. "With ye, though, it would've been me pleasure ta kill ye."

Out of the corner of his eye, Ian realized Aila was about to speak, but he motioned for her to wait. "So he wasn't good enough to marry your sister, but he was good enough for you to send here to spy on her?"

Fergus slowly rose with only his fisted knuckles still resting upon the table's top. "What are ye talking aboot, Mackay? I did nae send Lachlan here at all fer any reason. If ye saw him on yer land, it was nae by me order. I only ever sent two of me very most trusted men ta observe and report back ta me. I needed ta make sure me sister was being treated fairly, after all, did I nae? And if'n ye are accusing me of anything more, then we'll be having a problem."

Ian rose and faced him square on. "By your order or not, Lachlan Gordon did come to Borve Castle, and he killed one of my most trusted men and lost his own life doing it. The deed was done just outside the door my wife was sleeping behind."

All the color drained from Fergus's face. "I kenned Lachlan was angry 'cause ye ended up with Aila and nae him, but I'd nae ever guess he'd go so far as ta try and harm her. I truly am sorry for the loss of yer man. I owe him a debt I cannae ever repay if he gave his own life protecting me sister. Even if he was a Mackay."

Ian watched as a very tired Aila made her way across the floor and linked arms with her brother. "Are ye ready ta meet yer son then, Fergus? He's a bonny, hale and hearty lad ta be sure. Even if he was born in a stinking Mackay castle. He and Rhona are waiting above stairs for ye."

The poor man began to shake. "A son? I have a son? Truly? How am I ever gonna explain why he was born where he was ta me clan?"

Fergus's knees began to wobble, and he was more than a little unsteady on his feet as he headed up those stairs.

But Aila wasn't quite finished. "There be something else ye need ta ken, brither."

He stopped mid-step and hung his head. "I do nae ken if I can take any more of yer happy news this day, sister, but oot with it. Does he by chance have three eyes or completely be missing his nut-sack? I do nae care, I tell ye. Me son is me son and the next laird of the clan Gordon nae matter what bad luck being born on Mackay land has brought down upon his head."

She swatted him on the arm. "Ye hateful man. Yer son is well and whole. But yer wife had a hard time of it and cannae be moved for some time. Not ta mention that she promised me she'd attend me when my time comes. So do nae be upsetting her with talk of gathering yer men and riding out.

Ian groaned. He knew exactly what Aila was going to say next.

"Me bairn is still weeks away so ye best make yerself comfortable here at Borve Castle. Perhaps ye and Ian can spend some time together, become friends, since ye are now family."

Fergus scoffed. "I'm nae family with any Mackay."

She swatted him again. "Aye, ye are. Ye are me brither, and ye will be uncle ta all me bairns, which means when the time comes, ye will foster our sons just as we will foster yours."

Fergus's face turned an ugly shade of red. "Nae Mackay is ever going ta foster a son of mine."

Aila smiled. "Want ta bet? Rhona and I have already discussed it, and it's settled. Because if'n ye do nae agree, then I'll…I'll have nae but lassies, lots of them, each one worse than the one before it. And I'll send them all ta ye ta be fostered. I'll send them ta ye as soon as they're old enough ta wean. Perhaps even two at a time. And…and I'll even name one after ye."

Fergus turned a deathly white. "Nae. I'll do whatever ye ask, just do nae send me yer lassies. I barely survived the likes of ye. I'll foster yer sons, sister, and I'll allow ye and Ian ta foster mine. I swear it. Even though ye all be stinking Mackays. Are ye happy now? Might I please see me wife and bairn while I'm still young enough ta see at all?"

Chapter Twenty

Late December 1643
Borve Castle

"What're ye doing up there, laird?"

Ian glanced at Daniel from his perch in the loft and placed a finger over his lips, signaling for the child to be quiet. "I'm waiting for our lady," he whispered. "Now be gone. I don't want you giving away my surprise."

Daniel didn't move an inch. Instead, the little boy planted his feet even more firmly. "What surprise do ye have fer our lady? Ye best nae be jumping down and scaring her ladyship, me laird. She'll nae like that at all. Lassies don't, ye ken? Trust me, I learnt that one the hard way. And especially nae lasses with a big belly they've been toting around fer ever-so-long now."

The last thing Ian expected to do today was take marital advice from a child, but then Daniel did have a point. Scaring Aila was the last thing he wanted to do. On the contrary, if everything went as planned, the only screams his wife would be eliciting would be due to pleasure not fear.

Perhaps he should be waiting for her at the barn door when she came in to collect the eggs as she'd been doing for days now instead of the young girls assigned that duty. Even though the gathering of the eggs had always been their job.

And why weren't castle Borve's young ladies collecting the eggs as of late? Because they were much too busy tending to the never-ending needs of Castle Borve's month-long, unwanted guests, of course.

"Perhaps you're right, Daniel." In one quick hop, Ian jumped to the floor below. "But that doesn't mean you shouldn't be about your own chores."

The little boy stuck out his chin. "I do nae like stacking rocks, especially searching them out in the snow. I'm a guardsman. Ye said so yerself."

Ian sighed. "And a fine guardsman you are. But those fields won't clear themselves, and just like the rest of the Mackay lads, you're expected to do your share. That snow is barely more than a few flakes deep, and most of it has already blown away. Those big-ass stones need to be put somewhere out of the way. There'll be planting to be done come spring, and I certainly don't aim to be waiting around for the rocks to be moved out of the way then. Now off with you."

Daniel's shoulders drooped, but he did as his laird commanded. Ian watched him go, almost guilty for running the child off but at the same time grateful he was gone. He'd been planning this opportunity to get Aila all to himself for days, could almost taste her lips upon his and feel the heat of her bare skin against his.

His hands itched with the need to touch her, to hold her, and to caress every delectable inch that was his wife.

It'd been too long, much, much too long.

Especially since their bed and their chamber was still being occupied by Aila's brother and sister-in-law and would be for at least a few more weeks. By then, their own child would be born into this world. And the opinionated Gordon, his wife, and his brand-new son Callum would be free to travel back to Skelbo castle where they belonged.

But Fergus and Rhona still being at Castle Borve at the moment meant he and Aila had been left with no choice but sleep next to the fire in the great hall on a quickly put together pallet. That had meant cramped spaces, little rest, and absolutely no lovemaking in any way, shape, or form since many others slept in the hall and Aila was reluctant to show off that big belly of hers.

God, how he needed that kind of attention from his wife right now, and he was pretty sure she needed it, too. He'd caught her glancing his way more than once these last few days with that particular gleam of need flickering in her pretty green eyes. The sight never failed to take his breath away and make him rock-hard.

Yes, please, just one stolen hour with Aila all to himself. One hour not to have to share her with anyone else. Not her brother, not her sister-in-law, and not their constantly squalling infant. Let alone the cook, the serving girls, the butcher, the brewer, the baker, the sick, or at least a dozen others who seemed to think Aila Mackay was the one and only answer to all of their problems.

And then he caught a glimpse of her walking toward the barn out of the corner of his eye, and he held his breath in anticipation. The wind whipped at her red curls as she pulled her plaid close about her in an attempt to stay warm as the little egg basket swung to and fro.

His heart melted in his chest.

God, she was beautiful, but then simply beautiful didn't begin to do Aila Mackay justice. She was his everything, his morning, his night, his noon-time daydreams and midnight fantasies. She was his friend, his confidante, his wife, and his heart. And because of her and the feel of her small, warm hand resting against his as he slept, Ian no longer jumped from his bed and headed out into the darkness near as often as he used to.

She was home, his home, their home, and he finally felt as if he had truly come home from the war.

No longer did he think about leaving all the time or the promise Tobias had made him. Danny and his men would still be there to save long after his life with Aila was over, and that's when he'd take Fate up on his offer, and not a moment sooner.

Danny would understand.

Hell, Danny would even be pissed if that wasn't exactly how Ian felt, and he knew it. His best friend had been his best friend for a reason. They'd always had each other's back and each other's best interest at heart.

Ian's only regret was that Aila and Danny had never met. But then with time being the way time was, who really knew what the future might hold.

****

What was Ian Mackay doing, standing right dab in the middle of the wide-open barn door on a chilly winter morn? Didn't the daft man have anything better to do than stand about looking so devilishly handsome this early in the day with that cocky grin on his face and those big beefy hands fisted upon his hips as if he owned the whole world?

Slowly, Aila made her way toward him, her heart racing faster and faster with each step she took. It wasn't fair a man should be so bonny. It never had been. The fact that she hadn't been able to enjoy the benefits of having such a bonny husband for quite some time had been weighing heavy on her patience as of late.

Yes, she was huge with child, and yes, she was bone weary most of the time, but she was still drawing breath. She was absolutely sure that as long as she continued breathing, she'd continue craving Ian's touch, his taste, his smell, and everything else there was about the man.

She worried her lip. Yes, she craved Ian Mackay with every beat of her heart, but did he still feel the same for her? He hadn't demanded his husbandly rights for quite some time, not even so much as a quick rutting up against the pantry wall.

Was he perhaps finding comfort in another's arms? Someone whose belly didn't precede them into every room they entered.

Jealousy flared, and she tamped it down.

Who could blame Ian if he did look elsewhere? After all, no one had ever truly called her bonny and meant it, even on her best day, let alone now, when she was huge and tired and cranky all the time. Not to mention the fact her feet were so swollen and ugly she could barely force them into her shoes and that taking a deep breath had become nigh on impossible more than a sennight ago. Let alone sleeping through the night without getting up to relieve herself a half dozen times or more.

Her dander rose.

Aye, bonny she may not ever be, but she was still that grinning, handsome fool's wife and due at least a modicum of respect. Just as soon as she could waddle her way to his arrogant, bonny side, she was going to tell Ian Mackay precisely that in no uncertain terms.

By the time Aila made her way to the open barn door, she was fuming, and she'd just opened her mouth to give Ian the tongue lashing he so greatly deserved when he totally caught her off guard.

Warmth, like the rays of the summer sun, enveloped her as two big strong arms wrapped her in close and his mouth captured hers.

"I've missed you, wife," he whispered after deepening the kiss.

Tears threatened as her anger dissipated into the morning mist. "I've missed ye, too, husband. Sorely, I have," she whispered while kissing him back.

He tasted of Ian, fresh and crisp, cool and inviting, with just a lingering hint of warm Castle Borve's fine whisky upon his lips, and the sweet familiarity of it had her heart racing. She wanted him, and she wanted him now.

"Ian, I need," she cried. "Lord help me, I ken I'm nae much ta look at right now, and I'm as fat as one of those pigs ye brought back from Inverness, but I do crave yer touch so verra, verra much."

He held her at arm's length and tilted her chin until she was looking him straight in the eye. "Aila, you are the most beautiful woman in the entire world and throughout all time to me. I want no other, ever. I love you and only you with everything I am for as long as I draw breath and even beyond. And I need to make love to you right now. I really do."

He placed a hand gently on her expanding belly, and the babe inside moved, as if seeking its father's warmth just as she had. The thought made her smile.

"I love ye, too, Ian Mackay. I swear I do. And

though I really want ta make love with ye, too, with Fergus and Rhona still occupying our chamber, there is nae private place for us."

He cocked his head toward a layer of straw in one of the empty stalls and grinned once more. "This is private enough for me. I have a powerful need to be inside you, Aila."

Heat flooded her face and neck before traveling across her breasts and landing deep in the pit of her belly. "Here? Now?"

Ian nodded and winked. "Yep, right here, right now. No servants, no brother, no sister-in-law or noisy infant. Just me and you fucking our brains out for as long as we want."

She giggled. She couldn't help herself. "I ken ye are nae of this time, Ian. Truly I do, but Daniel is right. Ye do speak as if ye are titched in the head. We can nae be tupping in the barn, mind ye. It's nae seemly for a laird and his lady wife. It'd be," she hesitated, "like the farmer diddling the milkmaid and thinking nae one would be the wiser. Ye ken?"

This time he laughed out loud as he swooped her up into his arms and carried her toward the hay covered stall. "I'll gladly be your farmer, and you can be my milkmaid any day of the sennight. And I do not care who is the wiser."

Warmth, the likes of which she hadn't felt since mid-summer, filled her as Ian wrapped his arms about her and covered her from head to foot with his body, his hands, and his kisses.

Aila sighed and wiggled even closer into his embrace. Life in a drafty, still half-built castle left much to be desired in the middle of a Scottish winter.

Especially when delegated to a cold pallet on the even colder floor instead of a soft, warm bed.

"Am I too heavy?" he asked. "I don't want to hurt the babe."

She shook her head. "Nae. I like the weight and warmth of ye, but I must admit, with this big belly of mine, breathing is becoming quite a chore these days. I may need ta shift just a bit."

Before she realized what was about to happen, he flipped her over until he was flat on his back and she was straddling him. "Better?"

The sudden loss of heat was startling, and Aila shivered, but then an entirely new source of warmth took its place. The hard evidence of Ian's intentions pressed wonderfully against her cunny, and tendrils of excitement scampered down her legs and up her spine.

"Your turn," he whispered. "Ride me like the wanton woman I know you can be."

A heat that had nothing to do with the temperature of the barn filled her cheeks. "I am nae a wanton woman, Ian Mackay, and ye ken it well. I am huge with child and nae the least bit attractive."

"I think you are beautiful just as you are, and you can always be just as wanton if you want to be with me." He laughed. "Try it. I dare you. Be like those fey creatures you're always talking about."

The glorious sound of his laughter, the vibrations of it, went straight through her, tempting her to do as he said and be as naughty as he thought her capable of.

But could she? Could she really?

It was more likely that, if she tried, she'd look like a bloated whale straddling a poor mashed-flat elf than she'd resemble any kind of *silkie* or *kelpie*.

Still, Aila rubbed herself against Ian's long, hard length and watched intently as the man's eyes crossed.

Perhaps she could ride her husband as he asked. But then, isn't that exactly what any good Scot wife would do? She'd make a story of it to tell herself later. For Scots were nothing if not good story tellers. The *silkie* and the man from another time perhaps. The misbehaving *kelpie* or even the wanton *sidhe*? Something to make her smile while treating the sick or even gathering the eggs.

She grinned down at Ian while slowly sliding his kilt up and out of the way. Grasping his rock-hard cock, she rose and positioned his length at her opening. "If it's wanton ye be wanting, then it's wanton ye'll be getting."

Ian opened his mouth to say something, but Aila chose that moment to quickly slide down his shaft's length. Whatever he'd been about to say was lost in his surprised grunt.

That made her smile. Perhaps her husband was bonnier than she and perhaps he was worldlier, stronger, and knew much more about tupping than she ever would, but there was something to be said about this being on the top business. She recognized it was a position of power. A position he'd willingly given over to her. A position of trust, and she meant to be worthy of the honor.

Slowly, she rose up the length of him and then back down again. Over and over and over, faster and faster with each thrust. The thickness of his cock filled her, stroking her cunny from the inside out. It was a slipping, sliding, caressing, breath-coming-in-quick-little-spurts, frantic coupling.

She tried her best to prolong it. She didn't want it to end. She wanted to stay right here, right now, forever. She wanted to forget that her Ian wasn't really 1643 Ian Mackay at all. That he wasn't of this time. For just a little while, she wanted to believe he'd always be at her side and in her bed.

But would he?

Tears burned the backs of her eyes, but she knew he wouldn't see them even if they fell. His eyes were closed and his breathing rapid, so close was he to finishing. Any stroke now, and he'd fill her once more with his precious seed.

It was a filling she craved and a filling she meant not to miss worrying about things she had no control over.

With renewed vigor, she increased the speed of the strokes, glorying in the joining. The muscles of her cunny constricted to hold him in close while spasms of white-hot delight shot straight through her soul.

Aila felt his seed burst forth, warming her from the inside out. His cock contracted, his breath coming in quick little spurts, his body going rigid before finally relaxing. She held onto him as tight as she could, as if her arms grasping his shoulders and her legs snug against his thighs could somehow prevent his ever leaving.

She loved this man, and she believed with all her heart that her Ian Mackay loved her, too. But would that love be enough through the coming years to keep him by her side? To keep him from missing his own time and wanting to go back? She had to ask. She had to know, but at the same time, she was afraid to hear his answer.

****

Something was wrong.

His wife was now lying beside him with her sweet, plump ass against his hip, not moving an inch except for the up and down rise of her chest and protruding belly with each breath she took. Not that *that* in itself was a bad thing, for it wasn't. It was just that it wasn't what he'd expected at the end of surprising her in the barn.

If he'd done his job right, Aila should've been smiling up at him with mischief twinkling in her soft green eyes instead of facing away from him. After all, a well-satisfied woman would want to snuggle, right? He'd felt her sweet pussy contract around his cock, and he'd watched as a cat-licking-cream smile graced her full pouty lips the instant she shattered, but he couldn't help think he'd done something wrong. But what?

He gently turned her toward him and saw the tear tracks meandering their way across her cheeks. "Aila, what's wrong? Did I hurt you? Did I hurt the baby? Are you okay? I'm so sorry. I just thought. I mean, it's been so long. And I thought you wanted to, too."

She covered his mouth gently with her hand. "Ye did nae hurt me, Ian, or the bairn. And I did and still do want this. I am just verra pregnant and worried, is all."

He let out the breath he hadn't been aware he'd been holding and kissed her hand. "There's nothing you ever need worry about. I'm here, and I'll make sure you're always well taken care of. I promise I will."

Aila nodded. "I ken ye will, Ian. That is, as long as ye can. But what if that Fate fellow ye told me aboot comes back for ye? Will I wake some morn ta find ye gone?"

There was so much he needed to tell her and should've already. He should've told her all about growing up in Ohio and about his parents. And he sure as hell should've already told her about Danny and why he had trouble sleeping. And about the deal he'd made with Fate.

He had no doubt that he'd tell her everything someday. But not today. Not with her being this far along in her pregnancy and looking at him with such fear in her eyes. He'd not give Aila another reason to worry.

Instead, he smiled. "No, my love. You don't ever need to worry about me leaving. I made a deal with Fate, and he won't be coming for me until I'm ready to go, and as long as you live and as long as I live, I won't be ready to leave your side. Not ever. I love you with everything I am or will ever be, Aila Mackay." He rubbed her belly. "And I love our child, our home, and our people. I'm not going anywhere. I promise."

Aila smiled back at him. "I'll hold ye ta that then, Ian Mackay. Ye just wait and see if I do nae."

Chapter Twenty-One

Spring fifty years later 1693
Castle Borve Scotland

Ian glanced around the great hall at his family, all sharing their evening meal and smiled. It was an occasion that rarely happened these days. His oldest son, Brody, had been laird for close to twenty years, and when he wasn't out on the fishing boats like the man he'd been named for, he was usually still busy at supper time with the training of his men or the seeing to of so many other matters.

Castle Borve and the surrounding village had grown to the point that, very soon, Brody was going to have to share even more of his duties with his younger brothers, like it or not. No man was capable of doing everything by himself, not even one as stubborn as Laird Brody Mackay.

His brothers wouldn't mind a little more responsibility. He and Aila had raised all seven of their children to work hard and take care of their people.

Tobias, named for the pesky Fate who'd brought him to this time period, was the family rancher and took care of most aspects of the pig, sheep, and wooly cattle farming. Including the production, distribution, and sale of their quality wool surplus, smoked hams, and cured meats. While Stephen, named for Ian's Sutherland friend, was the farmer and responsible for the growing of the barley and oats and for the distilling of the fine Castle Borve *uisge beatha.*

Even old Fergus Gordon, before his death, had finally admitted there was no better whisky to be found anywhere in the world.

And then there was the quiet one, the scholar, Charles. He'd been named after the king who, though ultimately met his tragic demise at the end of a rope, had brought Ian and Aila together in the first place with his dictate that the Sutherland and Mackay clans be united in order to stop the feud.

Charles kept all the books and oversaw the finances for not only the castle but the majority of the entire village.

And a thriving village and seaport it was. The population alone had more than quadrupled over the last half century, and ships, cottages, out-buildings, and businesses could be seen clumped closely together along the coast and surrounded by fertile fields and grazing livestock for as far as the eye could see.

Not that his youngest two sons, the twins, Dougal and Daniel, cared a fig about the village or the crops or the smelly animals. They had much more important things on their minds. When they weren't chasing a pretty skirt. Though not yet quite twenty-five years, the two had already proven themselves worthy many times over on the field of battle. But then, with peace between the clans, for the moment anyway, perhaps it was time they found wives like their brothers had, settled down, and helped with the running of things.

Ian smiled as his eyes landed on Fergie, their only daughter, who'd been born in the middle of her six brothers. She'd been named for Fergus, after all, and that was okay. But their Fergie was the spitting image of her mother when Aila had been young. And not only did she look like Aila, but she'd also inherited her mother's skill as a healer. Though when riled, she could become as mean as an Ohio cottonmouth in the space of a single heartbeat. She had no problem holding her own with her brothers, either. She had each and every one of them just as firmly wrapped around her little finger as she did her dad.

Yes, she was amazing and certainly a delight to him in his old age. Even though he couldn't understand why she and her Sutherland husband, one of Stephen's many sons, felt it their duty to personally populate the earth. They'd brought five bairns into the world already and hadn't shown any inclination of slowing down.

Ian should be happy.

Bright, healthy grandchildren, and great-grandchildren climbed all over their still beautiful grandmother and scampered to and fro. The sound of laughter rang in the halls and spurts of contentment could be heard coming from every corner of the room. The sighs, the giggles, the animated conversations.

But all Ian Mackay could manage to feel this evening was tired, so very tired.

He took a deep breath and let it out slowly. God, how he still missed his best friend Danny, old Brody, Stephen, and even Fergus, though he'd never admit that to Aila.

At least he still had his best friend's namesake, Daniel. For close to forty years, Daniel Mackay had been head guardsman for the clan. A position he'd earned over and over again. Ian had no doubt that, this very moment, just like the wee lad he'd once been,

Daniel was out in the night patrolling the parameter of the Mackay lands, making sure no enemy crossed the boundary without his knowledge.

He chuckled. Oh yes, though no spring chicken, Daniel Mackay was for all intents and purposes the same today as he'd been the first time Ian had set eyes on him. Older for sure, wiser perhaps, but exactly the same heart and spirt.

God, to have even a spec of that man's tenacity and energy once again.

Ian stifled a yawn.

Yes, he was tired, but not just tired. He was sick and getting sicker. His chest ached more and more each day, his feet swelled, he was constantly short of breath, and a soul deep weakness had settled in his bones. It was getting harder and harder to hide his condition from his family, especially Aila, but still, he tried. He didn't want to see worry cross her lovely face.

After almost fifty summers in the highlands of Scotland and twenty-nine years in the twenty-first century before that, he was ready. Though he dreaded being separated from his wife and family for even a moment, he desperately wanted to finally have his chance to make right his one big wrong.

Not that anything was really up to him, though. For weeks now, he'd called and pleaded for Fate to come take him, but it was still right here and now where he remained.

"You always were an impatient one."

Ian's head whipped to the right. "Tobias?"

Fate grinned. "I told you I'd be back." He pointed skyward. "I simply had to wait for the right moment." He pulled the cell-phone-looking thingy from his pocket and started pushing buttons. "So I take it now's a good time, correct?"

Ian sputtered. "Now? In the middle of supper? With all my family gathered around me? Don't you think they'll notice if I simply disappear right before their eyes?"

Fate chuckled. "I think what they'll likely notice, eventually, is that you're no longer among the living at all."

Ian glanced down, and sure enough there sat his body, his cheek resting upon his arm just as if he'd fallen asleep at the table. But he could tell at a glance he was no longer breathing. It was the oddest sensation to know he was really and truly dead this time around, yet still feel so very much alive. He gulped twice, took one long glance at Aila, and then nodded at Fate.

As the air around him began to shimmer, he glanced back one more time to the woman who owned his heart, to his children, and his grandchildren before being sucked into the void.

****

A chill swept over Aila and her heart filled to overflowing with a cold emptiness, as if, even though sitting in the castle's great room filled with people she knew and loved, she was suddenly so very much alone.

Ian was gone.

She knew he was.

Felt it the moment he silently slipped away, and she didn't even need to glance in his direction to confirm it. Their bond had been that strong.

She looked down the length of the table at him anyway.

She couldn't seem to help herself.

His head was leaned forward, and his gentle, still-so-handsome face rested upon his crossed arms upon the table just as it had a hundred times before when he'd fallen asleep in the middle of their evening meal. It was not anything new, and no one else in the hall was paying the least attention to what was a common sight.

But Ian Mackay was not sleeping this time, at least not a sleep he'd wake from in a little while and smile up at her once more. He was dead, and her heart was breaking into a million pieces.

She was surprised and couldn't understand why she should be so upset. After all, she'd been expecting this day to come for some time now, dreading it, preparing her heart for the eventuality.

Over the last couple of years she'd made note of all the telltale signs that his life was perhaps coming to an end, and she'd treated each and every one as quickly as she could. Still, she wasn't anywhere near ready for the reality of a life without the man who'd stood by her side for nigh on fifty years.

Tears clouded her vison, and her throat threatened to close with the pain.

The children. How was she going to tell their bairns and the wee ones that their da and grand da was gone from them?

She glanced toward Brody, their oldest son and sighed.

Though he'd willingly taken his father's place as laird almost twenty years ago, he'd always had his dad's counsel to count on. That would be no more. And the weight of the clan's wants and needs would be even heavier upon his broad shoulders. As well as the pressure that would be put on Brody's oldest.

Wee Ian, named for his grand da, was but eighteen years and a few days old. But with the death of his grand sire, there'd be an even greater push ta prepare Brody's heir to take his father's place when the time came.

There'd be no more going where he pleased when he pleased or doing as he pleased for young Ian. No more roaming the Scottish isles or trying to best his cousins in hand-to-hand and sword combat. And no more teasing and tempting the lassies just because they were pretty. In other words, no more putting himself first.

From this day forward, young Ian Mackay's life would be one of service to his clan. She'd watched first her husband and then her son grow old, tired, and gray with the responsibilities of it. It was a cycle that never seemed to end.

And what of their other children?

Though Ian had taught each and every one of them to be self-sufficient, they'd never seen a time they had to do without him. But they would now. And hopefully they'd be able to fall back on the guidance and wisdom their father had bestowed upon them for when times got bad.

For life had a way of giving its share of ups and downs in fair measure.

But Ian going before her didn't seem the least bit fair to Aila's way of thinking. Not only was her heart breaking and her soul crying, but she was tired, so very tired. And she couldn't afford to be this tired right now. For there was now a funeral meant for a laird to prepare for.

First thing on the morrow she'd send a rider to

Castle Skelbo to inform Fergus's eldest son, Callum, and the entire Gordon side of the family that their uncle had passed. Then she'd send another south to the Sutherlands to inform Stephen's family of the same. And, of course, she'd send a third rider east to Castle Varrich to the Mackays stronghold and inform them as well.

And when that was said and done, she'd send wee Ian inta the village with an extra thirteen shillings and fourpence ta pay the bell ringer for his services.

Aila shuddered. The tinkling of the bell along the village streets and the declaring of the dead man's name for all ta hear had never been something she looked forward to. Then of course there was the cook to speak to about preparing the Lykewake feast, which would go on all week. And the after-the-funeral celebration of life to prepare for.

Ian had been loved by so many people. In the end, even Fergus, though the contrary old bloke would've never admitted it.

Aila felt her lips slip into an ever-so-slight smile. Yes, Ian and Fergus had made a real and true peace with each other over the years. She and Ian had fostered Rhona and Fergus's sons, all five of them, and they'd done the same for her and Ian. And both clans were stronger for it.

But even right up to Fergus's death two years ago, they'd still been miles apart as to who was on the right or the wrong side of the longstanding feud and who was not. Though, in the end, they did both agree that neither truly knew how the silly thing had started in the first place. They sometimes agreed depending upon how much Castle Borve's smooth *uisge beatha* they'd each consumed.

But they had become brothers, at least in a sense. Fergus had honed Ian's skill with a claymore, and Ian had taught Fergus to make and use black powder. Now they were both gone.

The smile left her face.

Soon she'd have to tell her children that their father was dead. And then, with Fergie's help, they'd prepare his body to lie in wait for everyone to arrive for the funeral. There'd be little sleeping to be had in the coming days.

It was custom to never leave the body alone lest the fairies snuck in and stole its soul. And this time Aila wasn't taking any chances.

She caught herself before she chuckled out loud. Fairies and *sidhe*s. Ian had never let her forget she'd thought him a *sidhe* at first. But then that had been before she'd found out he was from almost four hundred years in the future.

They'd had many conversations over the years about the time he'd been born in and the promise Fate had made him.

Was Ian back in his time now?

Was he this very moment in that dry, hot, desert place he'd spoken of so many times? The place he'd, even to this verra day, had nightmares about? If he was, would he be able to save his friend this time around like he'd saved her by coming back in time?

Aila wasn't a hundred percent sure she believed all the stories Ian had told her about the time he came from, like men walking on the moon of all things, flying in big machines across the sky from one end of the world to the other, and actually talking to people miles away through a little box-like thing they'd carry around in their pockets. She defiantly hadn't believed his stories, at first, about fire with no flame and light in the middle of the darkest night without the need for candles. He'd called it electricity. The stuff lightning was made of. He'd said, of all the things in the future, electricity, a well-made '98 Dodge pickup truck, and a hot, buttered cob of corn were the three things he missed the most about the land of Ohio, which was where he was originally from.

Unfortunately, there were also many things he'd told her that she didn't doubt for a minute. Like the fact men had not learned a single thing about getting along and were still just as mean and greedy and as apt to go to war as they ever were. Women still weren't considered quite the same as a man in many parts of the world but were still expected to work just as long and as hard anyway.

And even with all kinds of wondrous medicines to be had there was still death from so many diseases. And there was still hunger, intolerance, ignorance, and hate.

There were times she believed every single word he'd said and days she chose not to believe much of it at all. But one thing she never once doubted was, if there was any way possible for Ian Mackay to save his friend Danny and the other men he'd lost that day, then he'd do it.

Chapter Twenty-Two

That Day
Afghanistan

Ian opened his eyes and stared through the windshield of the Humvee at random people in strange clothing walking about, gesturing and speaking to each other in a language he couldn't quite comprehend. Somewhere, a child cried, dogs barked, an engine hummed, and an explosion went off in the distance.

He cringed and glanced at Fate who sat right between him and Danny in the vehicle. "So this is my chance to change what happened, I take it?"

Tobias Moiré nodded. "Your one and only, and you've earned it."

He gulped. He was young again and back in the middle of the Afghanistan desert on patrol. Danny was in the driver's seat once more, very much alive and smiling right at him, trusting him, laughing with the other men. Kent and Andrew were seated behind them with Ariel in his normal position as the turret gun operator.

A rush of joy overwhelmed him. He'd missed them all, but it was Danny his fingers itched to grab up into a bear hug just like the ones they'd shared sometimes when they'd been boys. It took all his will power not to do exactly that.

Danny wouldn't understand, and the others with

them wouldn't either. Not only didn't a staff sergeant show favoritism, but a staff sergeant sure as hell didn't go around hugging on his men.

Ian settled for taking in the sight of his best friend's smile and the sound of his laughter, knowing that if he could somehow pull this off and change what was about to happen, they'd all have plenty of time to catch up later.

He tried to swallow and couldn't. "Can they see you?" he whispered to Fate.

Tobias shook his head. "Of course not. Only you can."

Ian's mouth went dry as he sucked in a deep breath, his tongue stuck to the roof of his mouth, and his teeth felt so gritty they reminded him of sandpaper. Not that he really wanted to breathe very deeply anyway. Taking in a deep gulp of Afghanistan air this close to a village meant once more exposing himself to the cultural ambiance of diesel fuel laced with the odor of raw, human waste. Then that combination would mix with the smell of burning trash, oil smoke, dust from all the fucking sand, and whiffs of whatever spices were being used in today's cooking of whatever unfortunate animals they'd happened to have slaughtered in the last week or so.

Then of course the camels. How had he forgotten how rancid camels stank? The spiting, biting, piss poor excuse for horses still smelled like they'd been rolled thoroughly in fermented urine and baked until ripe in the hot desert sun for weeks on end.

Even with all four of the Humvee's windows securely shut tight, the stench of Afghanistan still managed to seep in. It was worse than he remembered, and he gagged.

Sheering those dumbass sheep season after season, fertilizing the fields with rotting fish guts, or rendering whale fat hadn't smelled half as bad as one freaking lungful of Afghanistan.

The hot sun bore down upon the vehicle and sweat trickled along his spine. What he wouldn't give to be in his kilt right about now instead of hot-ass fatigues. His heart pounded hard in his chest, and the desperate need to just grab Danny, jump from the Humvee, and run for the hills had his legs aching with the desire to do just that. But then he couldn't leave the other men who'd died that day behind either.

He knew exactly what was about to happen. He'd lived and relived this scenario at least a thousand times. Marines didn't leave a man behind. Not ever, not for any reason.

If only the Humvee would magically turn around just this once. They weren't supposed to be this far into this stinking village. Especially not in this particular section of this village. Right dab in the middle of a well-documented hot zone.

But they couldn't and wouldn't turn around. Of that, Ian had no doubt.

Like every other time before, the narrow dirt and gravel of the alleyway they were traveling prevented it. That and the freaking dogs, camels, and people meandering about the make-shift road.

Up ahead, he could see the intersection getting closer and closer. On both sides of the narrow, gravel street, people wandered to and fro doing whatever it is people do. Dogs barked, open market vendors sold their wares, and music blared. In a matter of heartbeats, men who'd been counting on him, and worst of all, his best friend in the whole world would be reduced to a mass of mangled bloody body parts strewn all over the fucking desert again, if he didn't stop it.

Not this time.

Not this fucking time!

Excitement filled him. He'd relived this memory so many times during his life in seventeenth century Scotland. He knew every single second of every single thing that was about to happen by heart. And he also knew no matter how hard he'd tired, he hadn't been able to change a thing. But this time was different. This time the outcome was within his power.

Even though he knew what was coming, still he startled as, just around the next corner, the snot-nosed little kid once more darted out into the middle of the road. His dark brown hair still hung limp in his dirty, little face. His eyes were still wide with fear. His ridiculously white shirt still hung wide open with the same row of C4 bricks all linked together with the very same red and black wires. The entire contraption was still strapped snuggly around his small torso. And just like before, the little boy was holding what looked to be a detonator in his tiny right hand.

Right on cue, Daniel poked him in the arm. "Damn, would you look at that, Ian? I can't run him down with those explosives strapped to him. Sorry, buddy, but you're gonna have to take the kid out."

The first second ticked by as Ian quickly lowered his window, and sighted down the barrel of his gun, but unlike the original incident, this time he could see right through the little boy and the surrounding buildings and tents and witnessed what was happening from not only in front of his position, but also behind and all around.

As another second ticked by, he realized that the detonator-looking thing in the child's hand wasn't really attached to anything so shooting the little boy wouldn't change what was about to happen in the least.

And by the time a third second had ticked off the clock, he saw the man he hadn't seen before standing on the top of a building well out of range. He was holding a mortar shell.

At the same exact moment, Ian watched in helpless frustration as an Afghani sniper popped out of seemingly nowhere and took out Ariel, the turret-gunner. It was that selfsame second that the mortar shell dropped into place.

He continued to watch in frustrated horror for the count of a little less than three more seconds, unable to do anything to stop what was about to happen. The mortar-shell launched.

Once again, the bomb went off. He felt the reverberations of it. But this time Ian didn't lose consciousness. This time the air around him shimmered and before another one of those horrible seconds could tick by, Fate had spirited him away.

With a whoosh, Ian found himself standing in a grassy meadow. "You fucking rat-bastard," he cried. "You knew all along I couldn't change a damn thing, didn't you?"

Tobias Moiré slowly nodded. "Yes, but I also knew you'd never believe me if I'd told you so. It was one of those things you had to find out for yourself."

"But why?" Ian shook his head. "I don't understand. Don't get me wrong," he shook his head again. "I'm grateful for the second chance you and your boss gave me. I've loved my life and my wife and my family in seventeenth century Scotland more than anything in the world. But why was Ian Mackay more important than Danny or the other men of my squad? Why did good men have to die while I got two completely separate lives? It's not right, and it's not fair."

Fate chuckled. "Fair? Who ever said life was fair? Do you really think your friend and your men were shortchanged a life? Just because you may not understand why things happen the way they do doesn't mean what did happen wasn't part of a much greater plan." He snapped his fingers. "But don't take my word for it. I think it's time you heard it directly from the source."

The air around them once more shimmered, and suddenly there were familiar faces before him. The very first face he saw belonged to none other than his childhood friend, Danny.

Ian grabbed him up in that bear hug, and his old friend laughed. "God, how I've missed you."

Danny hugged him back. "Missed you, too, bud, but I knew you'd be here sooner or later."

"I'm so sorry I couldn't save you that day," Ian whispered. "I would've gladly given my life for yours if I could've. I swear it."

He stepped back just far enough to see Danny's expression. He expected to see sadness, anger, or even regret, but the only change was his friend's smile got even bigger.

"Save me? From what? Do you have any idea what I do here?" Danny asked.

Ian shook his head.

"Do you remember when we were just boys and I got the biggest kick outta helping coach the younger kids?"

Ian nodded.

"Well, that's kind of what I do now. What I've been doing since the moment I arrived. I'm part of a group of mentors. We show the youngsters who come through the gate the ropes. You know, the kids who never really got a chance to grow up, because of illnesses, accidents, crimes, wars, or whatever. Even that little guy who had the bomb strapped to his chest that day. He's one of mine now."

Danny placed a hand on Ian's shoulder. "I wasn't cheated out of a life, my friend. I was simply given *my* forever opportunity a little sooner than some. I love what I do, and where I am, and I'd not change it for the world, and neither would any of these other guys."

Suddenly, three other sets of arms surrounded him in hugs as the faces of the other men who'd been in the Humvee that day came into view, and a feeling of peace filled him.

"None of us feel cheated, Ian." Danny smiled. "Kent's part of the group that's in charge of taking care of pets until their former owners finally arrive, and he leads the whole frigging choir now. And Andrew…" Danny chuckled. "You'd be proud of Andrew. He's chairman of the welcoming committee for babies who never had a chance to take a single breath. And Ariel…" Danny chuckled again. "I bet you'll never guess what Ariel does. He has the coolest job ever."

Ian looked directly at the man Danny was talking about. Ariel Cruz had been a young Philipino soldier who, though a master shot, had always seemed part psychic, too. If only he'd listened to Ariel the day of the attack. The young private first class had been very wary that day. To the point, Ian had almost left him behind. But he hadn't. Ariel was the best turret-gun operator in the whole squad.

Danny's voice pulled Ian out of his introspection. "Ariel's like a human dream-catcher, dude. He's part of an elite group who watch the still living's dreams and let the Boss know what their heart's desire is, so that when they finally do get here, what they've always wanted is already waiting for them."

The man Danny was talking about smiled at Ian and waved. "Best job ever. Thanks, man. Best job, best forever, best everything."

Tobias Moiré cleared his throat. "There will be plenty of time for getting reacquainted later. But right now, I'm fairly certain there are other people Ian would like to see." With the snap of his fingers, the air around them once more shimmered, and when it cleared, the meadow they were standing in was literally filled with people.

Ian was suddenly surrounded by familiar faces, and his heart filled to overflowing. Aila was the first new person he noticed. She hugged him so hard and for so long he almost felt like they were back home in Scotland.

"I know it's only been moments," he whispered. "But I've missed you, my heart."

She smiled right back at him. "Even a moment without ye was a moment too long."

And then standing right before him was wee Daniel, tall and strong and just as much a guardsman as Ian had ever seen him. Brody and Stephen and Fergus and so many other friends. Then all of his and Aila's sons and their daughter and their spouses. Their grandchildren and great grandchildren and so many other faces he didn't recognize but knew anyway. They were the children of his children's children and on down through the more than four hundred years since he'd first become a part of their family.

Together again, finally, and forever, never to be parted.

With Aila tucked against his side, Ian hugged them all and then looked back toward Fate and grinned. "Okay, I guess this does make up for not being able to change what happened. So then, what's my job to be? I'm ready to get to work."

Tobias chuckled. "Never let it be said the Boss doesn't have a sense of humor. You have heard about the size of the banquets we have around here, haven't you? So many souls to be fed? Apparently, the Boss thinks you'd make a right fine farmer."

Ian threw back his head and laughed. "A farmer for all of eternity it is then. You can tell your Boss it'd be my pleasure. I wouldn't have it any other way."

About the Author

Hi, my name is Maxine Mansfield and I write time travel and fantasy erotic romance. I live in the far northern state of Alaska where the summer days are long and the winter nights even longer. Welcome to my world.

~*~

Visit Maxine at
www.maxinemansfield.com

~*~

To chat with Maxine Mansfield and other Wild Rose Press authors of erotic romance, join us at
www.groups.yahoo.com/group/thewilderroses.

Also Available
from The Wild Rose Press, Inc.
and major retailers.

Time for a Highlander
Real Men Wear Kilts
By Maxine Mansfield

Forty-five-year-old history teacher Bethany Anne Anderson wasn't supposed to die on her Scotland vacation, but she's perfectly fine moving on to the hereafter. She has loved ones waiting for her. Then Tobias Morie, better known as Fate, steps in. Before she can move on, she must first help him correct one of his mistakes. That's fine until she wakes up in 1643 in the body of twenty-year-old Lady Elspeth Frasier. Worse, she's engaged to the very handsome, very young, very virile Quinton MacLeod. But that's not all Fate demands. She must give the Highland laird the heir he'd originally been denied.

Quinton MacLeod loved once. He won't do it again, even if he had time for such nonsense. With the Highland lairds divided between loyalty to their beloved country and the English king, he seeks only peace—in his keep and in his heart. But raised in England and a ward of the enemy, his beautiful new wife has strange notions of education and cleanliness that cause chaos within both. There's also the matter of her very unlady-like views on the marriage bed, which, come to think of it, he's more than happy to overlook. If only he could trust her.

Southern Rose

Gown & Dagger Seductions Book One

By Lily Bly

Rose O'Conner is a Confederate spy trapped among Union officers as the Civil War ends. When a Yankee from her past learns her secret, what is she willing to do to make him keep it?

Over the past year, Captain Grant Franks has searched for the alluring woman who stole his heart. When he learns she is a spy, will his dedication to the Union hold up against his desire for his Southern Rose?